KUDZU

John Mitchell Johnson

To Sudan

Best Wishes

John

5 - 19 - 18

Cover car photo by 1961Cometguy.

ISBN: 978-1-54392-817-4 (print)

ISBN: 978-1-54392-818-1 (ebook)

In loving memory of
Paul Brett Johnson
1947–2011

CHAPTER ONE

July 24, 1987

It was an awful day for a funeral, as if there could be a good one as Mamma Lou was fond of saying. The temperature was hovering around ninety-six and the humidity made the air feel as thick as the kudzu that choked the very life out of the Eastern Kentucky landscape. The air conditioning in my '81 Dodge Colt was blowing just a wee bit cooler than the outside air, but at least I could keep the windows up and keep my hair from blowing. Quite a trade-off, sweat for hair, but Mamma Lou always made a deal of a man's hair. It was the least that I could do today, have good hair. Mamma Lou liked the boys. And I guess the boys liked her.

The Colt strained and groaned at pulling the long grades of the Kentucky mountains, and each incline seemed to steal a little more cool from the already laboring air conditioner. The mountains were beautiful, and from the four-lane highway that traced the tops of the ridges, I couldn't see the mobile homes and beer joints and junkyards that followed the meandering paths of the county roads which lined the streams and valleys below. Except for the occasional horrible surgical scar from a long-forgotten strip mine operation, the mountaintops looked as peaceful and stately as sleeping lions.

I had left Nashville at daybreak. It seemed a lifetime ago. I had dreaded this trip for a while now, a journey I knew was looming. Nashville, Bowling Green, Elizabethtown, and Lexington, where I stopped for lunch: a Diego salad, Miller High Life, and an order of fried banana peppers at Columbia's. The peppers weren't as hot, the beer not as cold, nor the salad as crisp as I had remembered. Then Winchester, Campton, Jackson, and Hazard, and with each passing mile the dread building within me. It was indeed a bad day for a funeral, as if there could be a good one.

✳ ✳ ✳

July 8, 1962

"In that deeeaaaruh old village churchyard, I can see a mossy mound . . .

There is whereuh myuh mother's sleeping, in thee cold and silent ground."

Travis Wicker and I sat under the splitting mimosa tree in the side yard of Jonathan Waddles's house. Jonathan's wife Zelda could be heard wailing in sorrow above the mournful strains of the brothers and sisters of the Ball Branch Old Regular Baptist Church, or the

Old Regulars as they were called. The preacher was lining out the phrases to "The Village Churchyard," and those gathered echoed in high and lonesome responses.

Jonathan was laid out in the front room of their small home and the neighbor ladies had all brought in coffee cakes and potted meat sandwiches for his wake. Earlier that afternoon the funeral home had delivered a sixty-cup coffee urn along with old Jonathan, twenty-five folding chairs, and a box of fans on wooden sticks, picturing Jesus knocking at the door. The preaching and singing would soon be over and the neighbor women would wash up the dishes and say their goodbyes. The men would gather in small groups, drinking coffee and telling stories, as they continued the three-day ritual of "settin' up with the dead" while Jonathan lay corpse.

"If you don't do it you ain't got a hair on your lily-white ass," Travis said.

"I will if you will," I shot back. "Have you ever touched a corpse before?"

"Plenty of times," Travis said, without so much as a change in countenance.

"Your lying ass. Travis Wicker you've no more touched a corpse than you've seen Becky Thacker naked." The latter, another lie that Travis had perpetuated.

"I'll bet you I have. When my grandpa died I snuck in the front room about two in the morning when nobody was around, and I went up to the casket and reached in and got a hold of his hand."

"What did it feel like?"

"The thing I can best compare it to is a crocodile's belly. You know, cold-blooded and tough feeling."

"Horseshit, Travis. Now you're going to tell me you've felt of a crocodile's belly too? You ain't never felt of no crocodile's belly, nor no corpse's hand, and you ain't seen Becky Thacker naked. You're as full of shit as a burning porch poke on Halloween."

Mamma Lou was inside paying her proper respects. My older sister, Annie, was no doubt by her side, watching and listening as Lou held court over the body of a dearly departed neighbor. Lou wouldn't be singing with the Old Regulars. Lou had very little in common with them, for they wouldn't allow a woman to cut her hair, wear makeup, play the piano, or do many other things Mamma Lou was fond of doing . . . much less get married, divorced, and remarried. And Mamma Lou had a history of that.

Soon Mamma Lou emerged from the screened-in porch, Annie at her side. Lou dabbed her eyes with a handkerchief, attempting to absorb the tears while keeping the eye makeup intact.

"Lewis Ray, you and Travis get in the car," Mamma called.

Mamma Lou had named me, her second-born and what would turn out to be her only son, after herself. Why she didn't name Annie some variation of her own given name was beyond me, but I had come to be known as simply Ray or Lewis Ray, but never just Lewis.

Travis was pretty much a fixture at our house. Most of my friends' parents wouldn't allow their children to sleep over at my house, but Travis was the exception.

"Sweet Jesus, roll down them windows. This is a terrible day for a funeral," Mamma Lou lamented, "as if there could be a good one.

"It is some kind of hot this evening. They'll be lucky if they can have an open casket for the service. I thought Jonathan looked a little bloated already. It's hard to keep 'em up very long in this weather, unlike February when I had to bury Mitchell in the cold frozen earth. Oh my Lord, it seems like yesterday, and if I live to be a hundred I'll never forget the sounds of them blasting caps they had to use when they hit rock. Them booms echoed all over Stone Coal. God, that was an awful day for a funeral, as if there could be a good one.

"Shit it's hot in this car and my ass is sticking to this seat like it's flypaper. Travis, excuse my French and don't tell your mommy how I talk. I know I ought to do better."

Travis and I were too busy pondering our late-night return to Jonathan's house to be concerned with Mamma Lou's lack of decorum. Besides, it hardly merited an acknowledgement for it was as much a part of Mamma Lou as was the hair and makeup.

"I'm going to stop by Whip 'n Sip for a cold Nehi. Annie, do you want a Tab? I'll get you boys a snow cone."

"I'd rather have a Pepsi, Mamma," Annie said softly.

"I know you would honey, but you'd better have a Tab."

Later that evening, just as darkness was settling in the low lies of the creeks and valleys and fingering its way slowly toward the hilltops, Mamma came into the front room of our cramped trailer, obviously dressed for a night of carousing.

"You all don't think about leaving this house. I'll be back a little after midnight. If that nosey bitch Miss Haggard calls, tell her I'm at choir practice or something."

Mamma didn't look anything like she was going to choir practice. Annie and I knew she was going to Cooley's Nightclub over in Lothair. And a little after midnight usually meant two or three in the morning. At least that's what I had come to count on. Annie always did just as Mamma said and didn't leave the house . . . ever. I, on the other hand, took the opportunity to grow up way too soon. I knew things no twelve-year-old boy should know.

Mamma's car sputtered as she eased out of the gravel drive and onto the blacktop road. We lived in a rented trailer that was perched like a bird on a wire in a graded-out flat spot that overlooked Route 80 just west of Stone Coal.

As the last hint of day disappeared from the valley, I sat alone on the big rock at the edge of our yard. It was about the size of a couple of pickup trucks and was the perfect place to sit in the cool of the evening. Often Travis and I would camp out there. We would take our quilts and pillows and lie on our backs and stare at the sky. When Mamma Lou would turn the porch light off, the stars would look like a million lightning bugs. Sometimes Travis and I would pretend we were up looking down instead of down looking up. If you stared long enough you began to feel like you were going to fall right off of that rock and into the night sky. We would play a game, imagining where we would land if we fell off of the rock and into the sky. The rule was, when you fell into the sky you would turn upside down and do flip-flops among the stars until you got so dizzy you couldn't stand it any longer. Once you closed your eyes you would fall back to earth somewhere. Sometimes I would land over in Bosco or on top of Ball Mountain, or up on the High Rocks that overlook Stone Coal. Travis always landed in faraway places. He would land on the beach in Normandy where his granddaddy died or on top of the Eiffel Tower where he could see the White Cliffs of Dover in the far distance. Once, he landed in Rome on the tallest of the seven hills, and he told me how he saw the Forum and heard the clopping of the horses' hooves as the gladiators rode over the narrow cobblestone streets and into the Colosseum. Sometimes I felt embarrassed that the best I could come up with was the High Rocks, but I loved to hear Travis tell of all the places he would land. It was like I was with him on a trip, and then Stone Coal and Annie and Mamma Lou and the Whip 'n Sip and the Blue Star Grill and Uncle Wallace's Phillips 66 station would all become just a tiny speck on the world.

"Hey, turd. Are you ready to take the hand of the dead?" It was Travis's voice coming out of the darkness.

I sat bolt upright on the rock.

"You scared the living crap out of me. I didn't hear you coming."

"That's because I walk the night like a harbor fog and I light like a butterfly on a milkweed pod." Travis was a great lover of high drama.

"No, it's because you left your bike down by the road and you snuck along the ditch line and up the drybed and jumped out of the dark like a haint."

"Well, Lewis Ray, how about it? Are we going to go down to Jonathan's wake and take his hand?"

"I'm game, unless you're too chicken yourself." I sounded braver than I felt.

"I am Travis the Bravehearted from the House of Wicker. I fear no man, living or dead. So, if you're not too lily-livered, let the challenge begin."

"Okay," I said, "but I want to get the rules straight. Do we just touch his hand and get the hell out?"

"No way." Travis always made the rules. "We have to grab his hand and give him a handshake. And squeeze and hold it for a count of five."

"Holy crap!" I was feeling more uneasy by the minute. "This is getting too creepy."

"I knew you wouldn't do it. What do you want to do now? Go to my house and watch Lawrence Welk? Maybe *Mr. Ed* will be on, or are you scared of a talking horse too? Ooooh, Lewis Ray, you are so brave."

"Just shut up. We're going to Jonathan's and I'm going first. I'll grab his hand just like I's a fried chicken-eatin' Baptist preacher and I'll pump his old arm til it drops out of his shoulder socket." I was digging a deep hole and I knew it, but of all the things to be avoided in my life, none were greater than not measuring up in Travis's eyes. Although I didn't know it at the time, throughout my life this would repeat itself many times over. Travis was the springboard that made me embrace the challenge. Just like in the rock game, I would land in Bosco, but Travis would land in Rome. I wanted so much to land in Rome, and I wasn't really afraid of Rome, I just couldn't seem to see past Bosco.

By eleven o'clock we were on our bikes heading toward the home of Zelda and the late Jonathan Waddles. Though the night was dark and our Huffy bicycles had no lights, we knew Route 80 like the backs of our hands. Travis said we had sonar like bats. There was, however, just enough of a moon to allow us to navigate the road. At the big curve just before Jonathan's house we stopped and laid our bikes by the summer-dry culvert that ran under the highway. From this point on, our mission would be on foot.

We eased up closer to the house, making sure to stay out of the light until we could figure out a plan. Just like a couple of scouts on *Wagon Train*, we lay undetected in the darkness as we surveyed the lay of the land.

Four of the men were sitting in a disjointed circle under the mimosa tree in the side yard. The amber tint from the yellow porch light, specially colored so as not to attract bugs, cast an eerie hue over the scene. On the front porch two men sat drinking coffee and smoking cigarettes, their red embers serving as place markers in the semidarkness.

With the front and side entrances occupied, Travis and I strategized that we would have to gain entrance by way of the back door. We both knew the lay of the house and decided we would go through the kitchen, down the hall, and into the front room where Jonathan lay in repose. Since I had so stupidly insisted I would go first, Travis would stay at the hall door to keep watch, and if detected we would abort the plan and run like hell. If a breach came from the back of the house we would escape through the front door, and conversely, if one of the men on the front porch ventured in we would run out the back. If we had to retreat through the back, we would reconnoiter behind the pump house at the garden gate. If forced to exit the front, we would simply meet at our bicycles.

With such careful planning, what could possibly go wrong?

My heart was pounding in my chest and I could feel every beat in my temples as we skulked just outside the circumference of yellow light. Luck was indeed with us, for as we reached the perimeter of the back of the property, a long, thin, but very dark shadow fell across the yard, just the camouflage we needed to access the back porch. First Travis and then me. We paused for a moment with our backs up against the tarpaper brick siding of the house, steadying ourselves for our next move. My hands were trembling and I was getting my breath in little pants like a puppy on a hot afternoon. I looked at Travis and he was steady as a rock. I knew he would be. Not even a drop of sweat. He gave me the nod and I ever so slowly opened the screen door and slipped onto the back porch, Travis at my heels. The kitchen door was ajar and the room was empty and dark. The neighbor women had already cleaned up from the day's cooking and eating and had left for home.

We crossed the kitchen with deliberate steps so as not to disturb any creaking floor planks that might reveal our presence. The hall was dimly lit and was out of eyeshot from both the front and the side of the house. Travis was the first to make his way to the end of the hall, and then he waved me to follow, dramatically providing cover for my advancement. As I joined him, we peeked into the front room where the corpse lay. Just my friggin luck, the coffin was in an alcove and all that was in view from our perch in the hall was the foot end. This meant that I would not have eye contact with Travis when I approached Jonathan. Shit, shit, shit!

"You're on, buddy," Travis whispered. "When you get back I'll take my turn. Good luck."

Holy hell, I thought as I entered the front room. Looking around to confirm the room was indeed empty except for the dead man, I inched further away from the security of my partner Travis. I could now see all of the casket, but purposely didn't look in the open lid just yet. The funeral home had placed a lamp near the head, and it cast a peculiar orange hue. As I edged closer, Travis now completely out of my range, I took my first glance of Jonathan. My God, he was wearing a suit and tie. I had never known Jonathan Waddles to ever wear anything but overalls, even when he went to church. Most of the Old Regulars just wore work clothes to church, so why he was wearing a suit was beyond me. I wondered if it was bought just for the occasion, which seemed a waste at best. He looked old and skinny and orange. As I stepped again closer I began to doubt that this was Jonathan at all, but just some distant relative who bore somewhat of a familial resemblance. If Jonathan had teeth he never wore them, but now he looked like he was pursing his lips to cover buckteeth big as a mule's. His eyes were sunken and one appeared to have a crack that might pop wide open at any moment. The other one was glued tightly shut, and lo and behold, it looked like old Jonathan was wearing pink lipstick. This was the most macabre sight my twelve-year-old eyes had ever beheld. I looked over my shoulder hoping to see Travis, but all I could see from my point of view was the navy blue sofa and the pictures of Jesus and President Kennedy on the wall.

Maybe I could leave now, and just tell Travis I did it. But he would know. He could tell. Travis was that way. I bent over the casket. Here I was, just me and old Jonathan. I wanted desperately to look over my shoulder to see if Travis or even one of the men from the porch was behind me, but I couldn't take my eyes off Jonathan. Trembling, I reached toward the folded hands of the corpse. One hand lay atop the other, both resting stiffly on Jonathan's motionless abdomen. As my own hands got closer to those of the dead man's, every beat of my heart resounded so loudly that surely the men on the porch could hear the pounding. Flesh touched flesh and I withdrew like I had touched a Progress Red Hot woodstove on a cold winter morning. Slowly I reached again, until I had firmly laid my hand atop that of the cold stiff man in the casket. Then came the unwelcome realization that I would have to pry his hands apart to accomplish my task. Carefully I wedged a finger between the clasped hands of the dead Jonathan Waddles and began working my hand into the fissure. I continued to ply, and in what seemed like forever his hands gradually gave way with a waxy flexibility, and I was able to slide my open palm into his. I grasped with all the firmness I dared muster. Then it happened. Something moved. I looked at the cracked eye of Jonathan. Dear God, was he waking up? Was he getting ready to spew out whatever it was he was hiding behind those pursed lips? I could feel a presence in the room. I tried to release my grasp, but he wouldn't let go. Just as I opened my mouth to scream, I felt a mountain of a hand grab and hold tight to my shoulder.

"What the hell are you doin' you little dipshit?"

It was one of the men from the porch. Where the hell was my lookout? Where was Travis? As Jonathan relaxed his imaginary grasp on my hand I spun around to face my captor just as another man entered from the porch. About that time Travis yelled from the hall.

"Run, you son of a bitch, run!"

The men immediately turned to see where the yelling had come from, providing the distraction I needed to make my escape. I bolted to the hall and Travis and I tore through the kitchen and across the porch, nearly tearing the screen door off its hinges as we made our way to the pump house.

"Keep going!" Travis yelled as we crossed the garden.

Our bat sonar failed us . . . for in the darkness, just after we passed the far side of the garden, we both plowed squarely into the middle of Ball Branch, the muddy, silty creek that runs the length of the valley in which Stone Coal sits.

Squatting in the shallow water, we said nothing, but concentrated on trying to catch our breaths while keeping a lookout to see if the porch men were in pursuit.

"What the hell happened?" I finally found my voice.

"Partner, I couldn't see the front door. I was covering your back."

In unison we burst into laughter. Trying to stifle our gasps so as not to be detected, we sat neck-deep in the dark muddy water, gradually taking in what had just occurred.

"Lewis Ray Jacobs, you are the man!" avowed Travis.

He then slid his hand through the chilly water, and taking my hand in his he gave it a firm shake and counted to five. After what seemed to be a safe amount of time, Travis and I crept back through the garden to the rear of the pump house. The porch men and the yard men had united under the mimosa tree, coffee and cigarettes in hand.

"Who did you say them boys were?" asked a tall skinny fella in a Red Man baseball cap.

"Well, one of 'em was Lou Slone or Jacobs or whatever her name is now . . . it was her youngun I think, and the other belongs to Ada Wicker."

"What the hell that little son of a bitch was doin' reachin' in that casket is beyond me. 'Pon my honor, it seems mighty disrespecting to the dead. But I sure scared the shit outta that bastard."

"Well, what can you expect? Lou just keeps the roads hot, whoring around, and them younguns of hers are pretty much raising themselves. And poor old Ada ain't been right since her man got killed."

It was almost one o'clock in the morning when Travis and I got back to the trailer. We pushed our bikes up the gravel drive and stowed them behind the shed. Mamma Lou's car was still gone, so we just went over to the rock and lay there on our backs staring at the canopy of stars in the night sky until pretty soon I felt like I was up looking down instead of down looking up.

CHAPTER TWO

May 16, 1965

"Do you, Edwin Triplett, take this woman, Louisa May Slone, to be your lawful wedded wife? To have and to hold keeping only unto her, in sickness and in health from this day forth, as long as you both shall live?"

"I do," said Ed.

"And do you, Louisa May Slone, take this man, Edwin Triplett, to be your lawful wedded husband? To have and to hold keeping only unto him, in sickness and in health from this day forth, as long as you both shall live?"

"I do," said a beaming Mamma Lou, for the fourth time.

"Then by the powers vested in me as a lawfully sworn justice of the eighteenth judicial district of the great state of Virginia, I now pronounce you man and wife."

And with that Mamma Lou and Edwin Triplett became united in holy wedlock at the Misty Mountain Wedding Chapel in Clintwood, Virginia, I being the best man and Annie standing up with Mamma.

Most of the people I knew who were married in Clintwood were just a few years older than I, and the girl most often was pregnant. Mamma swore that wasn't the case. Travis had explained to me that the laws in Virginia were different than those in Kentucky, in that you could get married in one day. In Kentucky there was a two-week waiting period after you got your license before you could actually get married, thus the young expectant couples would often rush to Virginia.

"Well here we are, one big happy family," Mamma Lou gushed as we loaded back into Ed's 1960 Dodge Dart.

"Doesn't it feel good to all be together?" Mamma asked over the seat as Ed backed out of the parking lot. "We're going to be so happy, I just know it."

"It feels real good, Mamma," Annie obediently replied.

I reserved comment for now. I hardly knew Ed Triplett. I had seen him at Uncle Wallace's Phillips 66. He would hang out there in the evenings with the other men who had nothing better to do. They would swap knives and lies under the pole light in the side lot until Aunt June, my dad's half sister, would flash the porch light to the upstairs apartment over the filling station, thus indicating it was time for Uncle Wallace to lock up and come for supper. The few men that were gathered would get in their cars and trucks and head for home or to the next loafing spot. In the winter they would gather around the coal stove inside the filling station and Aunt June would stomp on the floor at the appropriate time.

"Let's stop by Dawahare's and look for Lewis Ray a sports jacket and then we'll go out for a wedding supper before we head back to Kentucky. Don't that sound like fun, everybody?"

Yeah, Mamma Lou, that sounds like a real blast, I thought. I was getting a new sports coat so I could take Annie to junior-senior prom at Bosco High. Annie had much rather stay home for her junior prom than to be escorted by her brother, but Mamma Lou wouldn't hear of such.

"Honey, you've got a pretty face," she would tell Annie.

"And when you lose some of that weight you're gonna get you a boyfriend. Just wait and see. No way you're going to set at home in that trailer reading *'Teen* magazine and eating Moon Pies while all the popular girls are at the prom. Lewis Ray can be your date. We can go over to Pikeville and get you a prom dress. Dion's has sizes for big girls. We'll go to Carol's Cut and Curl and get your hair done up real pretty. Honey, you all'll split that prom wide open. You go in there just like you own the place. Make sure Lewis Ray dances with you a few times and pretty soon them stag boys will be coming around to your table like cows to a salt lick. You'll be hitting that floor dance after dance with a different feller every time, and them town girls will be settin' there with their thumbs up their asses just staring at their boring old boyfriends. Honey I found out, you don't have to be the prettiest or the smartest or the thinnest to be popular with the boys. You just got to find what works for you," Mamma said, perhaps more to herself than to Annie.

So that's how we ended up in Dawahare's on Mamma's wedding day, with me trying on every sports coat that would remotely fit a fifteen-year-old boy who was too gangly for the men's clothes and too tall for the children's. Mamma settled on a double-breasted navy blue jacket with light-gray pants, a baby-blue shirt, a red tie, and a red handkerchief for my lapel pocket. Mamma reinforced many times not to blow my nose or wipe my hands on the handkerchief. It was only for looks.

As I stood in the mirrored alcove that allows you to see yourself from way too many angles, I looked for all the world like an adolescent version of Mr. Howell on *Gilligan's Island*.

After a wedding supper at the Alpine Inn in Pound, Virginia, we finally arrived back at the trailer at about midnight. Mamma and Ed had bought the trailer and the lot on which it sat from Willard Terry, a well-to-do businessman who most people considered to be a bit of a shyster. He owned the hardware store and Stone Coal Grocery and Feed, two of our town's more successful enterprises. He had let Mamma and Ed buy the trailer and lot on a land contract. Willard being the richest man in Stone Coal was a lot like a sow being the prettiest pig in the hog lot; the bar was set low.

The week before the wedding Ed had finished adding a bedroom and a bath to the back of the trailer for him and Mamma, and I had gotten Mamma's old bedroom. The best thing about that is the way the window faced the highwall behind the trailer, I could sneak out late at night and sit on the rock and look at the stars. There wasn't actually a whole lot of sneaking to it because nobody seemed to know or care. Sometimes Travis would creep in the window after I had fallen asleep and jump straddle of me and start riding me like a palomino pony. I would rear up addled and confused and start flailing my arms wildly to fend off the unknown intruder. Once I came somewhat to my senses, Travis would cap his hand over my mouth to stifle the stream of cuss words that had come gushing forth. Then he would fall over backwards onto the floor in a fit of laughter.

At last, the night of the prom arrived, and I had just gotten my prom outfit on when Travis came in through the window.

"Don't you ever think of knocking?" I asked.

"At the window? Why on earth would I knock at the window?"

"Well I don't know, it just seems like you should let somebody know you're there. But I guess anyone who would sneak in your room and pounce on you like a bobcat while you're sound asleep couldn't really be expected to knock in broad daylight."

"You look pretty enough to kiss, Lewis Ray. Come over here and give your old buddy a little sugar."

"Screw you Travis," I said.

"I wasn't going to go that far, but you do look awfully sexy."

Travis then walked over to me and snatched the red handkerchief out of my jacket pocket.

"I've got a riddle for you, Lewis Ray," Travis said.

"I got no time for riddles and give me that handkerchief back."

"Hickory dickory docket, what does a poor man throw away and a rich man put in his pocket?"

"I told you, Travis, I don't want to hear a stupid riddle."

"Go ahead, try to solve it. What is it that a poor man throws away and a rich man puts in his pocket?"

"I don't know, money?" I asked, trying to appease Travis.

"Money!" Travis exclaimed. "Why would you say money? That doesn't make any sense. Why would a poor man throw away money?"

"I don't know. Why would a sane person ask a stupid riddle?"

"I'll tell it to you one more time. Hickory dickory docket, what does a poor man throw away and a rich man put in his pocket?" Travis continued, waving the red handkerchief wildly in the air.

"I told you I don't know. Now give me my handkerchief back before Mamma Lou comes in here and kicks both our asses."

"I'll give you a hint then," Travis said, taking the handkerchief to his face and making a honking sound as if he were blowing his nose.

"What are you doing?" I cried in disbelief.

"I'm giving you a hint." And he repeated the repulsive pantomime.

"Give me my handkerchief," I demanded.

"Do you give up?" Travis asked as he stuffed the handkerchief back into my pocket.

"Whatever," I said.

"Snot."

"What?"

"Snot."

"What snot?" I asked in exasperation.

"That's what a poor man throws away and a rich man puts in his pocket. Snot."

"Travis, what in the hell are you talking about? Why would a rich man put snot in his pocket?

"Haven't you ever been down at the Phillips 66 when one of the old farts needs to blow his nose? He walks a few steps from the crowd and turns his back and then pinches off his nostrils. Then he'll blow a big string of snot out and sling it on the ground and wipe his hand on his pants leg. One time after Wallace had just done that, he got his knife out and peeled and cut up a big Red Delicious apple. He asked me if I wanted a bite. As bad as I did, I just couldn't get him slinging that big snot string out of my mind."

"I guess you're trying to tell me a rich man picks his snot back up and puts it in his pocket?" My irritation was becoming more evident.

"No, stupid. A rich man carries a handkerchief, thus he blows his snot in his handkerchief and folds it up and puts it back in his pocket."

"And that's supposed to be more sanitary than slinging it on the ground?" I queried.

"Dumbass, it don't have anything to do with sanitary. It's a friggin riddle. I don't know why I waste my breath on you Lewis Ray."

"Well it's a stupid friggin riddle. About snot."

"Leeewis Raaay," Mamma called from the living room. "Are you about ready? I've got the Kodak and a new roll of films. We need to snap some pictures while we still have good light."

Just as I was turning to answer Mamma, Travis planted a big kiss across my mouth.

"My God, you're handsome." Travis bolted toward the window.

I kicked at his rear as he jumped from the windowsill, but only got air.

"Hey, Lewis Ray," Travis poked his head back in the window, "it's a good thing you're doing. You know, taking Annie to the prom. You're alright." And then he was gone.

✳ ✳ ✳

"Well Lewis Ray . . . you look absolutely handsome. I mean it, handsome!" Mamma Lou beamed.

"Lordy, I have birthed some good-looking children," Mamma Lou continued.

"Wait til you see Annie. She's as beautiful as any girl who ever come off of this creek. We couldn't get into Carol's, but Christy Bates gave her an updo this afternoon and she just looks absolutely gorgeous. Come on out here Annie and let us all take a good look at you."

When Annie came down the hall from her bedroom and entered the small cluttered living room, I could see what Mamma was talking about. Annie did indeed look beautiful, and far beyond her seventeen years. Annie's steps were unsure and her gait was awkward, but I could tell she was pleased with the way she looked. It was a shame, I thought, that such a pretty girl had to go to the prom with her little brother.

"Annie, you look real good," I said, not knowing exactly how to tell her how pretty I thought she was. Annie had always been attractive. She had a lot of Mamma Lou's features, but they were softer and more subtle on Annie. I had often thought that maybe Mamma had started out that way, but now life had left her with an edge. I know it had been hard on Annie to live in Lou's shadow.

"Now Annie don't you take that toile wrap off, I don't care how stifling it gets in the gym. It covers some things the good Lord gave you too much of."

Mamma had a way of saying just the wrong thing at the very wrong time.

"Come on children, let's go out in the yard and snap some pictures. Ed, get the camera. I'll take the films in to the Rexall next week to be sent off."

Annie and I obediently posed in the front yard as Ed followed Mamma's instructions on picture taking.

It was almost dark when Mamma and Ed dropped us off in front of the gym at Bosco High.

"We'll be back at twelve o'clock sharp," Mamma said. "We might go over to Cooley's for a little while, but we'll be here when the prom lets out. You all have a big time. I'll swear I have good genes. Just look at them good-looking children."

With that, Mamma Lou and Ed cruised out of the parking lot and left Annie and me standing in front of the gym to figure the rest of it out for ourselves. Neither of us had ever been to a prom before.

"Let me look at you," Annie said, straightening my boutonniere. Mamma had gone to Flo's Yellow Rose and picked me up a red carnation for my lapel buttonhole and Annie a white and red carnation wrist corsage.

"I guess you'll pass, for a skinny little hillbilly," Annie kidded. "Seriously, Lewis Ray, I'm sorry you had to do this. You know I'd much rather stay home and watch TV than be here, and I know you got better things to do."

"What do you mean? How many ninth-graders get to go to the prom? Zero, except for me. All's I'd be doing would be hanging out with Travis and getting in trouble. Now let's go in there and show them that our white asses would make any of them a Sunday face." I wasn't sure exactly what that meant, but Mamma Lou said it all the time and it seemed appropriate for the occasion.

We didn't exactly split the prom wide open and the boys didn't exactly fall all over themselves asking Annie to dance, as Mamma Lou had predicted, but all in all it was okay. I danced with Annie a few times and despite our attempts at practicing at home, we were a bit stiff and stilted on the dance floor. But we were there, and as much as Annie protested, I think it was important to her.

As the night wore on, an eleventh-grader named Jerry Conley started hanging around our table. He said he and Annie had study hall and American History together. He did his imitation of Mr. Sparks, their history teacher, which drew polite laughter from Annie. Just as the prom was about to wind down, Jerry asked Annie to slow dance. Timidly, they took to the floor, and after a few awkward toe-stepping incidents they began to smooth out, and I sensed that maybe for the very first time Annie claimed a little piece of herself that night. After the song was over, Jerry placed his hand gently in the small of Annie's back and walked her to our table. He smiled tenderly and pulled her chair out for her as she took her seat.

As the band was packing up their instruments and the prom committee was taking down the crepe-paper streamers, we stood and moved toward the door, and Jerry leaned in and ever so lightly pecked Annie on the cheek.

"Thanks for the dance," he said.

Annie blushed.

Mamma and Ed were patiently waiting in the parking lot when the prom was over, and Mamma wanted to know every detail on the ride back to Stone Coal. Of course there wasn't a whole lot to tell, but Annie and I tried to make it as interesting as possible.

"Mamma, Jerry Conley sure seemed awfully interested in Annie tonight," I said, giving Mamma something to grab on to.

"He did not," Annie replied, "he's just a goofy boy who does a poor imitation of Mr. Sparks."

"Whose boy is he, anyway?" Mamma Lou inquired, her ears perking up like a Chihuahua puppy.

"I don't know, but he lives down at the mouth of Triplett Branch," I said.

"Ed, do you know Jerry Conley? Whose youngun is he? Your people all live on Triplett Branch," Mamma continued.

"I think he's Dave Conley's son. He delivers groceries for the Cash and Carry after school and on Saturdays. He seems like a pretty good boy to me."

"Well I just think that's mighty fine," Mamma said, "here you are at your first prom and you got yourself a feller."

Annie gave me the look. The look we both understood. The look that said, "See what you've done now?" I returned Annie's look and shrugged sheepishly in apology.

"Mamma, one dance hardly makes him my *feller* as you say, and besides, I've got bigger and better things in mind for me than a delivery boy from the market."

"Honey, I did too," Mamma said, wistfully, as she looked blankly out the window into the night.

"What the hell is that supposed to mean?" Ed, who was usually as flat as a johnnycake, piped up.

"Well honey, it just means that there's good times and bad times in a person's life. And believe you me, I've had plenty of both. But just look where I am now." I sensed Mamma's thinly disguised attempt at damage control. "Happily married to a handsome man, two beautiful and smart children, and I own my own trailer. So it looks like the sun is shining on this dog's ass today, don't you think, Ed?"

"I suppose so, as long as you're the dog's ass." Ed replied with an uncharacteristic hint of humor.

When we arrived at the trailer Mamma went into great detail on how we were to hang our clothes. Although I didn't realize it at the time, Annie and I were wearing a substantial investment, money that Mamma could ill afford to spend. After I had changed into a pair of cutoff jeans and a worn tee shirt, I joined Mamma and Annie at the kitchen table. They were munching on some stale popcorn and sharing a sixteen-ounce Tab, poured over ice.

"Mamma, tell us about your senior prom," I said as I pulled a chair up to the dinette.

"Lord honey, that seems like a lifetime ago. And in some ways it was. You all don't want to hear about that. It's ancient history."

"I didn't know you went to the prom, Mamma," Annie said. "Tell us about it."

"Well, I thought it was the most fanciest thing I had ever seen. The juniors had decorated the gym for us seniors. The theme was *An Evening in Paris*. They had built an Eiffel Tower out of chicken wire and tissue paper. Mr. Lawson's manual-training class had made the frame, and the decorating committee had stuffed each one of those little holes in that chicken wire with a tissue-paper square. They had taken black crepe paper and made a fake ceiling and had stuck shiny stars to it. I thought to my soul that this must be the very way that gay old Paree looked."

"Did you have a date, Mamma?" Annie asked.

"Well, I imagine I did. Your daddy took me to the prom. He was the handsomest thing I had ever seen. I caused a bit of a fuss because the principal didn't want to allow me to bring him, him being two years out of high school. But them town girls always brought older boys who used to be on the basketball team or such. Your daddy didn't exactly fit that mold. But anyhow, I pretty much told them to kiss my ass. If the town girls could do it honey, Louisa May Slone could do it. I'll never forget my mommy settin' me down before the prom and having a talk with me, you know, about the birds and the bees. Well she didn't know it at the time, but that little talk was about a month late . . . and I was too," Mamma continued with a dismissive laugh. "I guess you all are old enough to know some of that stuff."

"What did Dad wear?" I asked, changing the direction of the conversation.

"A white sport coat and a pink carnation, honey just like in the song. And he was a looker, I'll tell you. You know, I'll bet he still is. Lewis Ray, sometimes you look to be the spitting image of him."

Mamma Lou had always joked that she had been married three times and in love twice, but only once with a husband. I figured that husband was my daddy. That was of course before Ed, but I figured the only thing that Ed impacted was the number of trips to the altar. We'd seen this before, and though Ed seemed nice enough, I knew better than to get too used to him.

Spring soon gave way to early summer and early summer to dog days. Ed and Mamma seemed to be happily wed, or as happy as Mamma ever was with a man. Over this time I had come to like Ed. He really didn't seem to contribute much, but he was a stable force in our otherwise unpredictable lives. When Mamma was married to Leonard Greene, a very brief and uneventful espousement, Leonard took us all to Saint Petersburg, Florida, to visit his sister. That was the only time I had seen the ocean, and I remember standing in the surf for the first time. With each new wave that washed over my feet, my footing became less and less stable, until I had to move and find another place in the sand on which to stand. Life with Mamma was often like that. With each new start, the footing felt more secure than the last, but soon the sands began to shift.

Mamma had started calling in orders for groceries from the Cash and Carry so Jerry would deliver to our house. Never let it be said that Mamma Lou failed to work all the angles. At first, Annie would make herself scarce when Jerry was around, even though he would tarry and look searchingly over our shoulders. Occasionally Annie would come into the room and say hello, and then quickly retreat. However, persistence paid off, and by late summer Annie and Jerry could be found sitting on the rock in the corner of the yard enjoying the cool of the evening. A car date was a long time coming, but it eventually happened and by Labor Day Annie and Jerry were an official couple.

CHAPTER THREE

School started back the last week of August. It was the hottest time of the year and the old stone building at Bosco High smelled of mold and old schoolhouse after being shut up over the summer. Annie was a senior and Travis and I were beginning our sophomore year. It felt good to no longer be the underest of classmen, and on the first day of school Travis and I vowed to find some freshman and try to sell him a used study hall manual. Of course, we ourselves still had a little bit of trepidation over the story the sophomore boys told us last year. It was sworn that before a boy could begin sophomore Phys Ed, he had to undergo a shot in his left ball with a square needle. We were pretty sure that was just a story made up to scare the freshmen. Pretty sure, but maybe not as sure as we would like to be.

Jerry Conley had his own car now and most mornings would come by and pick Annie up. They were good about allowing me to tag along. There was nothing cooler than arriving at school in a car and nothing more uncool than riding the faded old yellow bus.

Jerry played on the basketball team and had practice every day after school, so Annie and I had to ride the bus most evenings. My heart would ache as we rode past Joe Kilgore's restaurant, an after-school hangout where all the in-crowd would be eating fries and listening to the very best jukebox in the whole world. Joe never put any Loretta Lynn or Bill Monroe hillbilly crap on his jukebox like the one at the Blue Star Grill in Stone Coal. Joe's jukebox had the Beatles and the Rolling Stones and Herman's Hermits and Wilson Pickett. Travis rode the bus as well, and most evenings we would hang out at the Whip 'n Sip before going on home. Annie, of course, went straight home and did her homework. If there were clothes to be washed she usually took care of that too. Mamma and Ed were becoming more and more scarce, especially since Ed had taken a job at the Piggly Wiggly working evenings.

Travis and I had sophomore English and Health and Phys Ed together. The first few weeks we only had the Health part of the combination class, leaving us time to ponder the accuracy of the shot in the ball story. Romey Nobel became so concerned that he actually asked our teacher, Mr. Stanley, if the story were fact. True to his nature, somewhat funny and mostly cruel, Mr. Stanley hedged.

"Now boys, there are certain things that you all are going to have to do in this world to become men. And some of them aren't very pleasant. I'll just say this much, Miss Erhler, the school nurse, has got hands big enough to palm a beach ball. So once she gets a hold of you and comes at you with that needle don't you even think about running or she'll grab you and squeeze them things so tight you'll have the stone aches for a month. It's best just to buck up and take it."

"Mr. Stanley, are you just messing with us?" Romey inquired.

I had been in class with Romey since elementary school, and he was never recognized as being particularly intelligent. On the contrary, after repeating the first, second, and third grades, he was passed on from year to year due to the futility of having him detained. Also, he was now approaching his nineteenth birthday and only a sophomore.

"Nobel," Mr. Stanley asked, "have you ever masticated?"

At least seventy-five percent of the class saw what was coming, but the other twenty-five percent, including Romey, began to squirm and look at their shoes.

"What's the matter?" Mr. Stanley continued. "There's nothing to be ashamed of. I'll bet most of the boys in here have masticated. It's just part of growing up. Now Romey, level with us, do you masticate regularly?"

"I'm going to tell you the truth," a red-faced Romey replied. "I've done it a few times, but I don't make a habit of it."

A ripple of snickers and giggles went across the class, coming from both those in the know and those who, like Romey, were clueless.

"Well, when you do masticate, where do you do it?" Mr. Stanley continued.

"I'd really not want to say."

"Nobel, there's nothing to be ashamed of, like I said."

"Well, once I was doing it in the bedroom, but my mammaw caught me, so I've done it in the bathroom ever since, cause there's a lock on the door."

The entire class erupted in laughter, except for Travis, who just looked out the window and held a blank stare.

Later that afternoon on the bus I took my usual seat by Travis near the back.

"That was a good one that Mr. Stanley got on Romey," I began.

"Yeah, that was friggin hilarious," Travis shot back.

"What's with you? What are you so uptight about?"

"Lewis Ray, what's so funny about some poor dumbass not knowing the difference between jacking off and chewing? And Mr. Stanley has got to be the sickest old bastard in the world to pull that shit. Romey Nobel is nineteen years old and in the tenth grade, for Christ's sake," Travis said, "and Mr. Stanley is supposed to be a teacher."

Suddenly I felt small and ashamed. I hated it when Travis saw those things that I wish I had seen. He never had the need to laugh just because everyone else was laughing, or to wear what everyone else was wearing, or to listen to the music everyone else was listening to. And the thing I hated most of all was looking bad in Travis's eyes. But he always knew when I felt like I was coming up short. And then it was Travis to the rescue. This reassured me in one sense, but somehow made me feel worse.

"Oh hell, it's really no big deal. How about you, Lewis Ray?" Travis said as he thumped me on the shoulder with his fist. "Have you ever masticated? Or were you too busy pounding your pud, choking your chicken, massaging your short leg, playing peekaboo with your little buddy?"

"Travis, you're crazy."

Kudzu

※ ※ ※

Although the fall days seemed to creep by, before I knew it, Christmas break was upon us. We had survived the semester with no hypodermic needle to our genitals, however, we had told all the freshman boys what a horrible ordeal it was and whatever you do don't try to run, lest Miss Erhler snatch your balls near clean off.

Four days before Christmas we got our first big snow of the winter, probably six or eight inches. The snow seemed to somehow mitigate the dreariness of the short days and barren landscape of the winter mountains. The night of the snow Mamma Lou had gone out, probably to Cooley's, but she hadn't really said. Ed was likely at his job at the Piggly Wiggly in Bosco. Since Thanksgiving he had had to work late most days. Annie and I were alone in the trailer on the hill, and we watched out the window as the valley took on the snow. It was almost magical to see the junk cars and trash piles disappear under the blanket of pure clean white. Occasionally a car would creep by on highway eighty, but it seemed as soon as it passed its tracks would be covered, restoring the pristine facade created by the falling mantle.

Just before ten o'clock I made out headlights rounding the curve east of the trailer. As they came closer to our house I could tell the car was going to try to navigate our drive. Finally I was able to see it was Ed's Dodge and he was picking up speed in an attempt to gain enough momentum to make it to the trailer. About halfway up the hill the tail end of the car began to fishtail to the right, then the left, and finally the Dart seemed hopelessly stuck. Ed abandoned the car and made his way to the front door on foot, nearly going down on more than one occasion.

"Damn," Ed said as he came through the door shaking the snow out of his hair, "it took me nearly forty-five minutes just to get back from Bosco. Where's your mamma? Her car's not here," he added, stating the obvious.

"She left about dark, just as the snow started," I replied. "Said she was going to run some errands."

"Shit," Ed cussed. "Errands my ass. She ain't called has she?"

"No, the phone lines went down about an hour ago. I was on the phone to Travis and they just went dead."

"Shit!" Ed said again as he put his coat back on and headed out the door.

The Dart was sideways across the driveway and Ed struggled for nearly fifteen minutes before he was finally able to back down onto the road and head toward Bosco. The lights in the trailer flickered as Ed's car disappeared in the snow.

Annie and I decided to pop some corn while we still had lights. The television line had gone down before the phones did.

"Where do you think Mamma Lou is?" Annie asked.

"I just hope I know where she ain't," I replied.

"Where?" Annie asked. "Cooley's?"

"Ed don't know it, but Cooley's might just be the least of his worries," I mused.

"Don't talk like that, Ray. You don't know where Mamma is," Annie said.

"Right you are, Annie. I sure don't know where Mamma is. How about going out and getting us some snow in that dishpan? I'll make us some snow cream to go with our popcorn. Be careful now, and don't get any yellow snow."

"We don't have a dog, Lewis Ray. The only way we'd have any yellow snow is if you've been peeing off the back porch again." Annie kidded as she picked up the dishpan.

It was about midnight when the electricity finally went off, apparently to stay. We had a gas heater in the front room and Annie took the couch and I curled up with a favorite blanket on the worn settee. We could hear the occasional crack and snap of a limb as the weight of wet snow brought down trees out on the ridge.

"Lewis Ray, do you ever wonder what's to become of us?" Annie asked just as I was about to drift off to sleep.

"Don't worry, Mamma will be back in the morning, as soon as the highway department gets the roads cleared," I assured her.

"That's not what I mean, Ray. What's going to become of us? I'm a senior in high school. I've never had a real boyfriend, unless you count riding to school and eating lunch with Jerry. I'll be graduating in May and I've got no future. I don't want to sit up here on this hill in this godforsaken trailer for the rest of my life. And how about you? What are you going to do? You can't spend the rest of your life running up and down the creek and hanging out with Travis."

"Annie, tomorrow will take care of itself. Just get through today. I try not to think of what's to become of me. When I do I just always come up short. Travis dreams big dreams, Annie, but he's got no better chance of getting out of these hills than we do. You'll find a good man. It may end up being Jerry, and a girl could do a lot worse. You'll get a job over in Bosco and have babies and Mamma Lou will be a grandma and you'll be okay. We'll all be okay."

"But Ray, I want more. I don't want to work at the Rexall over at Bosco and I don't want a bunch of snot-nosed kids, and I sure wouldn't want Mamma Lou to warp them like she's tried her best to warp us."

"I guess Mamma has done the best by us that she could. It's all we've ever known so it doesn't seem quite so strange. At least she's not like Ada Wicker. Poor old Travis has to live with everybody knowing his mom is crazy as a shithouse rat. Mamma's not crazy, she's just different."

"Maybe for you, Lewis Ray, but I've never been pretty enough or thin enough or smart enough. You talk about coming up short. That's all I've ever felt around Mamma. She's been too busy marrying and divorcing and dating and being Lou Slone."

"Annie, let's just go to sleep. At least we're warm and got food to eat and a roof over our heads, even if it is rusty aluminum. When the daylight comes things will look different."

"If you say so, Ray. If you say so."

Morning came and there was no sign of Mamma Lou or Ed, and there was still no electricity, phone, or television. Annie had a transistor radio and we were able to pick up WKCB in Bosco. We were hoping for some music, but all that was on was Tradio on the Radio and local obituaries. With so many phones out Tradio was pretty slow. Willard Terry called in and said that he had plenty kerosene, canned hams, and tire chains at the Stone Coal Hardware if anyone needed them. He would also deliver in his four-wheel-drive truck for a small fee. With calls being so slow, Bud Rogers, the deejay, played several records by local bluegrass gospel bands to fill the time. Most of the listening audience probably thought this was just fine, but it was too painful for Annie and me, so we decided to save the batteries for later when Buzz Doolin would be playing rock and roll.

The snow finally stopped late in the afternoon, and as evening fell over the valley Annie and I started the second dark, but warm, night, with still no sign of Lou or Ed.

Then morning came and with it the beginning of the thaw. It was the day before Christmas Eve and I awoke to the sound of running water, which at first I feared was a broken pipe, but turned out to be the melting snow running down the sides of the trailer. Just before noon the lights flickered a few times and finally came on to stay. I was getting ready to bundle up and walk to Travis's house when I heard Mamma Lou's car in the drive. Annie came to the living room and we watched out the window as a very disheveled Mamma got out of the car and headed toward the door.

"Don't say a word, Annie," I admonished, as Mamma Lou entered the trailer.

"Hey kids," a subdued Lou said, "wasn't that snowstorm a bitch? Sorry I couldn't get home, but I knew you all would be okay."

"Have you seen Ed?" Annie asked.

"Yeah, I seen him," Mamma said as she headed for her bedroom. "I'm tired and I'm going to bed. You all keep it down so I can rest."

Christmas came and went that year with little fuss. Mamma and Ed never spoke of the events of the snowstorm, but Annie and I knew there was a storm brewing inside of Mamma. As the bleak days of winter settled upon us we could sense that the coming spring would herald a rebirth of sorts in our mother. And that was seldom a good thing.

CHAPTER FOUR

July 24, 1987

Just as I crossed the Pratt County line I began looking for the exit that would take me to Mill Creek, a small community of four hundred or so about eighteen miles from my final destination of Bosco. I would make time for another stop. As I rounded a gradual, sweeping curve at the foot of Ogden Mountain I spotted the access road that led down to Mill Creek. At the foot of the ramp and directly across old Route 80 sat the Dixie Drive-In, a well-kept cinder block building with overhung eaves that at one time were trimmed with a continuous ribbon of neon. In my youth, the graveled parking lot would be packed with automobiles sitting side by side waiting for the carhops to bring their orders of Dixie Burgers and fries, but today mine was the lone car in the deserted lot. The neon sign in the window read " pen." The "O" had been burned out as long as I could remember. The screen door creaked a familiar greeting as I entered the restaurant, and a tall oscillating pedestal fan stood in one corner of the dining room stirring the humid afternoon air. The same worn red swivel stools as from my memory lined the lunch counter. An unmistakable Gracie Dixon was bent over the counter sink washing up a few dishes, probably ones left over from lunch. She was stooped, wrinkled, and completely white-headed, but unmistakably Gracie.

"Can I hep ye?" Gracie asked, as she continued her chore.

"Yes," I said, "I'd like a grape Nehi and a piece of pickled bologna."

"Honey, I'm out of Nehi and I don't carry pickled bologna no more. I've got a couple of pork tenderloins left over from lunch or I can fix you a burger," Gracie said, still not looking up from her dishes.

"I said, I want a grape Nehi and a piece of pickled bologna, and I want Gracie to skin it back for me," I demanded.

Gracie looked up slowly and a grin began to spread across her face revealing a trademark gold tooth. Gracie had once confided in me that she actually wore dentures but had the dentist put a gold tooth in front to make them look more natural.

"They ain't but two boys on the face of this earth I ever let get by with any bad talk in my restaurant. Come over here Lewis Ray and let me get a look at you. I ain't heard nobody ask for that in many a year."

As I stepped closer, Gracie came from behind the counter drying her hands on her apron.

"Well Lordy mercy, Lewis Ray Jacobs you are a sight for sore eyes. 'Pon my honor. You're just as good-looking as you were when you was a teenager being chased by the girls. You and Travis were

Kudzu

something else. Whenever I seen one of you I seen the other. Yall were like beans and taters. Bend down here and give me a hug."

"Gracie, you haven't changed a bit," I kidded, as I nearly picked her up with my embrace.

"The heck I ain't. I used to be a fairly pretty woman, but honey I seemed to have broke once I got old."

"Gracie, you're only as old as you feel," I replied.

"Lord, don't say that. I feel like s-h-i-t," Gracie said, spelling it out.

"Well you look good to me," I said.

"Well just don't look too close," Gracie replied.

"I was thinking about you just this morning," she continued. "I was wondering if you'd come in for the funeral. Lord it's a hot one. Some of them was talking in here yesterday wondering if you would come in. I figured you would."

"Well, I'm not there yet, but that's where I'm heading."

"They said there was a good crowd at the wake last night. I don't suppose I'll go. You know I don't drive any more. I hardly do more than walk from the house out here to the restaurant and back. You knew Opp died didn't you? He's been gone near four years now. I was married to him for forty-seven year and fussed with him near every day. I miss that old s-h-i-t," again spelling it out. "He was a good man."

"Gracie," I smiled, "there'll never be another like you."

"We had some high old times in this little roadhouse didn't we? I remember that New Year's that you came in here. Travis and you

43

had words. I thought you was going to fight. Lord, that near broke my heart. And all over some little feisty-britches that, in my opinion, wasn't good enough for neither one of you. I probably shouldn't be saying that. Do you remember?"

"I wish I could forget."

"Them days are gone forever," Gracie continued. "Once they put the new four-lane in, Mill Creek has pretty much dried up. I still open for lunch every day. A couple of crews from the state highway department stop by for the special and I still have a few regulars from off the creek, but most days I'm closed and back to the house in time for my afternoon TV stories.

"You remember that night you and Travis talked me into hiring a band? Lord, we must have had a hundred people crammed in this place. Cars were parked all up and down the road and Lori Martin called the law cause somebody was blocking her driveway. That old biddy couldn't drive and didn't even own a car. I don't know why she got so lathered up about her drive being blocked. Dallas Wright was the High Sheriff at the time and he came down here acting all high and mighty saying how he was going to close us down."

"I had forgotten all about that, Gracie. How did you get him to leave us alone?"

"I took him in the back room and told him I'd give him a few free lunches. I pointed out that there was no drinking going on. You know I never allowed any drinking or bad talk in my restaurant. I also pointed out that everybody knew that his sister-in-law, Dakey Reynolds, was bootlegging over at the Blue Star. If he could turn a blind eye to bootlegging in his own family it seemed to me that he could let a bunch of younguns have a dance. And I also give him five dollars to shut up and leave." Gracie cackled as her eyes disappeared in her smile.

"Well, I'm getting ready to lock up," Gracie continued. "Won't you walk out to the house with me for a spell? I'll fix us a glass of sweet tea. It's a lot cooler on the back porch where the breeze comes out of the holler."

"I'd like that, Gracie. I'd like that a lot."

✳ ✳ ✳

The summer of 1967 was my seventeenth. My first priority that summer was to get my driver's license, and against Mamma Lou's wishes, I did just that. Shortly after the previous Christmas, Jerry Conley had convinced Grady Smith to give me a job at the Cash and Carry as a stock boy in the afternoons and on Saturdays. I had managed to save nearly every penny I made in hopes of buying myself a car by the summer. Grady paid me one dollar per hour, cash money, and most weekdays I could work at least three hours and get in six or seven on Saturday. He and his wife Louise used to work open til close, but as they had gotten older and a little more financially secure, they had taken to going home early and leaving me and Jerry to mind the store. I primarily stocked the shelves and carried the trash out back and burned the boxes down by the creek. Jerry tended the register and helped the customers up front. If he got a delivery then I would watch the front until he got back. Though Grady and Louise's house faced the side street, it was actually attached to the store by a hallway from the feed room, so they were always available if I ever had a question.

By the time my birthday arrived I had saved four hundred and sixty-eight dollars and was officially in the market for a car. Opp Dixon, who along with his wife Gracie owned the Dixie Drive-In over in Mill Creek, had a 1961 Mercury Comet in his drive with a For Sale sign on it. Mamma Lou and I had driven by it a couple of times, and at my insistence we finally had stopped to ask about it. But Gracie had explained that Opp was not at home and she didn't know much about the car, other than she thought he wanted five hundred and twenty-five dollars for it.

"Good lord, Mamma, I've got almost enough saved up to buy that Comet," I exclaimed as we drove away.

"Well honey, *almost* only counts in horseshoes and dynamite," Mamma responded.

"What the hell does that supposed to mean?" I asked impatiently.

"Watch your damn mouth, Lewis Ray. It means you ain't got enough money to buy the car."

"Oh God, I wish I did, Mamma."

"Well honey, wish in one hand and shit in the other and see which one gets full," Mamma continued.

"Good lord, Mamma, could you speak English for a change? Why would I want to shit in my hand, anyway?"

"Watch your mouth Lewis Ray. It's just an expression."

"How about you loaning me the rest of it Mamma? I will work every chance I get and give you every penny I make til I get it paid off," I pleaded.

"How about you work and save every penny you get and then buy the car? And you could buy some groceries and pay the light bill too since you seem to be so rich."

"Mamma, it won't be there much longer. It's a good car and Opp Dixon has taken care of it like it was a baby. Please, loan me the money," I begged.

"Well sure Lewis Ray. I'll just pull off the road down here at the straight stretch and see if I can't snatch forty or fifty dollars outta my ass."

"Well, how about Ed, Mamma? You think Ed would loan me the money?"

"Shit, Ed don't have a pot to piss in or a window to throw it out of, more's the pity. You'd think anyone who didn't marry til he was in his forties and lived with his damn mommy all that time would have something to show for it. I hit the jackpot this time didn't I?" Mamma said, more to herself than to me.

A week later I was at the Dixie Drive-In with what I hoped was a plausible plan.

"Mrs. Dixon," I said as the thin dark-haired lady with the gold tooth approached the counter. "I notice your husband, Opp, still has the Mercury Comet for sale in your driveway."

"It's Gracie, honey. And yes, it appears that Opp still has the Comet for sale."

"Well," I continued, "I'm here to make you a proposition."

"Well, now just who are you?" Gracie asked politely.

"Oh, I'm sorry. I'm Lou Triplett's boy from over on Ball Branch. You may remember my mother as Lou Slone or Lou Jacobs."

"Oh yeah, you all were by here the other day. Yes, I do recall your mother. And your father too. They used to come in here when they were not a whole lot older than you. Lord, they were a good-lookin' couple. And I see they had a good-lookin' youngun too. You favor your daddy a right smart. Opp and I were never blessed with children, but I feel like I raised half the younguns in this county, you know, that's hung out here over the years. I guess they've been my children. I've tried to keep a good place for them to hang out. I've never allowed any drinking or bad talk or disrespect. I will say, you appear to have awful good manners." *For being Lou Slone's boy*, I guessed may have been the rest of that sentence.

"Thank you ma'am, er, Mrs. Dixon. About my plan?"

"Gracie," she interrupted.

"Well, Gracie, I have four hundred and sixty-eight dollars saved up from working at the Cash and Carry in Stone Coal, and I want more than anything in this world to buy your husband's car. I am offering to give you that money today. Right now. I will work for you here at the restaurant for the going rate to pay off the balance. I would need to hold out five or so dollars a week for gas, but the rest you could keep til the car was paid off."

"Okay, supposing I was interested, what do you know about the restaurant business?"

"Absolutely nothing." I hoped Gracie would appreciate my logic. "But I didn't know anything about the grocery business until Grady Smith gave me a job at the Cash and Carry. Now I can open and close, run the register, operate the slicer, wait on customers, take out the trash, and anything else that needs doing."

"I like you," Gracie said, revealing the gold tooth. "You've got grit in your craw. Grit will take you a long way in this old world. Opp and I started with nothing and have scratched out a decent living in this little roadhouse. Of course, me being barren, we ain't had to support no younguns. And Opp has a regular job, too."

"Yes, ma'am," I interrupted, "how about my idea?"

"Well, what about your job at the Cash and Carry? You plan to leave Grady and Louise high and dry?"

"No ma'am, I've already thought about that. My best friend is Travis Wicker, Ada Wicker's son. He is needing a job and Grady says he will hire him to take my place if I were to get this job."

"Poor old Ada. She took it awful hard when her husband got killed. She ain't never been right since then has she?"

"I guess not, ma'am. So how does my idea sound to you?"

"You're like a hog rooting for an acorn ain't you? Well, I'll have to talk to Opp. It is his car, after all. You come back a Tuesday and I'll let you know something."

"Yes ma'am, thank you ma'am, I'll be back on Tuesday," I said, hardly able to contain my excitement at the prospect of owning the Comet.

The next few days seemed to crawl by, but finally, on Tuesday afternoon I had Jerry Conley give me a ride to the Dixie.

"Come on in," Gracie said as I entered the restaurant. "I think Opp's out to the house. Let me latch the door and we'll go see if we can find him."

Gracie latched the front screen of the drive-in and, after putting a Back in 5 Minutes card in the window, motioned for me to follow her. We went through the kitchen and out the back door. A narrow, worn path with an occasional and random stepping-stone led from the restaurant to the back porch of the Dixons' home next door. Opp was sitting on the edge of the porch with a lawn mower turned upside down and its innards scattered about him, half-glasses perched low on his nose.

"This is the boy I was telling you about, Opp. He's Lewis Ray Jacobs, Lou's boy."

Opp was a rather small balding man, and what hair he had was a fuzzy mix of red and gray that only graced the sides of his head.

"What do you know about lawn mowers?" Opp asked, as he looked up from his work.

"Not much, I'm afraid," I confessed.

"Me neither," Opp said with a smile. "I guess I know enough to tear it apart, but I'm afraid I don't know enough to put it back together. The only good thing about that is it was broke before I started in on it. Oh well, Gracie tells me you want to buy the Comet," Opp continued.

"Yes sir, I do," I said with great sincerity.

"She also says you're a little shy on the money end."

"That's right, sir, but I'm willing to work it . . ."

"I know," Opp interrupted. "Gracie told me your plan. Here's how I've got this figured. I ain't much on the restaurant business. Matter of fact, I pretty much avoid it. That's all Gracie's. I pretty much keep to myself. I work on the broiler and the plumbing and I keep the weeds cut and the parking lot picked up and I paint and gin around wherever Gracie needs me, but my main job is working for the Kentucky West Virginia Gas Company. It's Gracie's restaurant, and she allows how she could use a boy like you to help her out. Actually, Gracie done took money out of the restaurant and paid me for the car. So the deal you've got is between you and Gracie. The car's yours but you owe Gracie the down payment of four hundred and sixty-eight dollars. That leaves thirty-two dollars, which she is going to let you work out."

"But the car costs five hundred and twenty-five," I said.

"That damn woman jewed me down on my own dad-blamed car," Opp said with a laugh.

"Come on, son," Gracie piped up, "we need to start teaching you about the restaurant business."

※ ※ ※

I began blowing the horn at the foot of the dirt road leading to Travis's house. I was hoping Ada wasn't home because I knew that any commotion upset her, but I couldn't hide my exuberance. As the Comet came to a screeching halt in the dusty drive, Travis emerged from the house wearing no shirt and blue jean cutoffs, with an RC Cola in hand.

"What in the hell?" Travis exclaimed.

"I got the car!" I yelled through the half-open window of the Comet.

"Well hell's bells," Travis shot back.

"So what do you think?" I said, getting out of my newly acquired pride and joy.

"Well it ain't no Corvette Stingray, but it beats the heck out of a bicycle and it's a damn sight better than what I've got. Which is nothing."

"Really," I continued, "it's pretty cool isn't it?"

"It is indeed," Travis agreed, as he went around to the front of the car, kicking the tires and looking intently at the vehicle, as if he had any knowledge whatsoever of automobiles. Finally, holding his RC Cola high in the air as if to offer a toast, Travis proclaimed, "You fine automobile, previously known as Opp Dixon's Comet, will now and forevermore be known as Lewis Ray Jacobs's Vomit. I now christen thee."

With that, Travis upended the bottle of RC and poured it over the hood of my clean, newly waxed car.

"Oh hell, Travis," I said, "you've got friggin RC all over my car and what's worse the name Vomit will stick like glue."

"Indeed it will," Travis said. "I plan to see that it does. Now, if you will excuse me, I'm going to put on a shirt and shoes and we are going cruising."

Our first stop was Uncle Wallace's Phillips 66, where, after putting two dollars worth of regular in the tank, we pulled into the bay and washed the RC from the hood of the car.

We spent the rest of the afternoon driving from Stone Coal to Bosco to Mill Creek back to Bosco and finally back to Stone Coal. We had the windows down and even the thick mountain air somehow felt fresh and light. We had the radio on full blast and life had never been better. All was good.

Just as the sun was beginning its descent behind the mountains and the humid air was taking on the first hint of the evening cool, Travis looked at me with an all-too-familiar glint in his eye.

"I've got an idea," he said. "A very, very, good idea."

"Oh, hell," is all I could say.

"Hear me out."

"Travis, hows come every time you get a good idea I end up in a hell of a mess?"

"A hell of a mess or a mell of a hess, you must admit it's always an adventure," Travis replied.

"Yes it is, my friend. But not even you can screw up today, so what is it you have up your sleeve?"

"Let's throw a party. Why don't we go over to the Blue Star, buy some beer, and go up on the strip mine roads and build a bonfire?"

"We're not old enough to buy beer, Travis," I replied. "We are only seventeen."

"Lewis Ray, you are so friggin stupid. Dakey is a bootlegger. She don't care how old you are. Do you think she's going to want to see your ID, for Christ's sake?"

"Travis, you're going to get me killed one of these days."

Thirty minutes later we were at the Blue Star trying to look cool and collected. We had devised a plan of action on the drive over. We would go in, take a seat in a booth, play a few tunes on the jukebox, and order a couple of Cokes. The Blue Star had jukebox stations at each booth, which would make it easier for us to blend in. Travis and I weren't exactly the usual Blue Star patrons. We were definitely more of the Whip 'n Sip crowd.

We had just gotten our Cokes when Linda Hudson slid into the booth beside me.

"Hello, handsome." Linda smiled as she nestled against my arm. "I don't see you two around here very often."

We had been in the same class as Linda since fourth grade, even though she was a year older than Travis and me. She lived in Four Mile, the next small town down Route 80 from Stone Coal. I never did know what Four Mile was four miles from, in that it was about two miles from Stone Coal and eleven on to Martin. Linda was somewhat of an enigma, one of those girls who really didn't fit into a mold. She was in all the advanced classes at school, but hung out with the kids from the slow classes. I thought she was as pretty as any girl at Bosco High. Prettier in many ways. She hardly used any makeup and tended to wear faded Levis and flannel shirts. She had been in trouble a few times at school, but nothing more serious than skipping classes or smoking in the bathroom.

"Hey, Linda," I responded. "What's happening?"

"It's Stone Coal. Nothing ever happens," Linda said.

"Well this is your lucky night," Travis interjected, "because we are getting ready to buy some beer and go up on the strip mine roads and build a bonfire. It's party time! So if you want to hang out with two cool and handsome guys, you just go out there and wait in Lewis Ray's Vomit and we'll join you in a moment."

"Who are the two cool handsome guys?" Linda asked. "I guess you and Lewis Ray will have to do," she said, laughing as she moved toward the door.

Shortly after Linda left the restaurant, Travis approached the counter.

"Whaddaya need?" Dakey asked, a Lucky Strike dangling from the corner of her mouth.

"I need eight Tall Boys," Travis replied.

"What makes you think I would be able to help you with that?" The cigarette was bobbing up and down as Dakey talked.

"I am Travis Wicker, Ada Wicker's son, and I have lived on this creek all my life and I know you could help me out."

"Well, you hand me over four dollars and you go wait by the back door and I'll see what I can do."

And just as Travis had predicted, in a couple of minutes Dakey handed a brown paper bag out the back door of the restaurant, into Travis's eager arms.

"Got it!" Travis said as he returned to the car. "Where's Linda?"

"Probably got a better offer," I responded.

Just as we were about to leave the Blue Star I spotted Linda at the pay phone in the corner of the parking lot. I pulled the Comet up to the phone booth.

"Need a ride, cutie?" I yelled out the window.

As Linda hung up the phone Travis jumped over to the back seat, hoping Linda would join him, I assumed. But instead she opened the front door and slid across to my side.

"Drive, handsome," she said. "I was just calling a few friends to tell them there's a party at the strip mine tonight."

Abandoned strip mines had become unauthorized recreational areas for teens in Eastern Kentucky. A network of neglected dirt roads followed the contours of the mountaintops and meandered and intersected like a burlap bag full of black snakes. The banks on the sides of the roads closest to the ridgelines were honeycombed with huge auger holes where the remaining coal was bored out after the flat area had been stripped. The opposite shoulders were vertical drop-offs that fell steeply to the valleys below. These cliffs had claimed more than a few young lives—drivers, after a night of drinking, had often failed to negotiate the unmarked and unpredictable twists and turns of the strip mine roads. Deserted mining operations had left behind a dichotomous landscape. Horribly disfigured and barren terrain was surrounded by the lush and verdant Appalachian forest, and occasional retention ponds provided clear cold reservoirs of mountain water.

The Comet groaned as it pulled the steep grade of the access road leading up to the summit. As we reached the crest and headed west into the maze of trails, the sun slipped behind the last tall mountain in the distance.

"I told everybody to meet down by Yellow Creek Road," Linda said. "Do you know where that is?"

"I'm going to guess it's where the access road from Yellow Creek comes up," I replied.

"You're not only good-looking, you're smart too," Linda said.

"Yeah, he's sharp as a needle-dicked dog," Travis piped up from the back seat.

"I think if I just follow this road and keep bearing to the left we'll get there," I said, and all agreed.

After a few miles we rounded a sharp turn and spotted a couple of cars, one of which I recognized as belonging to Johnny Frank, a kid from school whose annoying manner could challenge the patience of Job.

"Hey dickhead, come and help us get some firewood," Johnny called, as we got out of the car.

"He's talking to you, Travis," I said.

"Very funny, Vomit Boy," Travis shot back with a smile. Soon we were all gathering wood for the bonfire.

As evening turned to night more cars gathered at the mine and the fire became the focal point of drinking, singing, and telling of wild stories. A couple of boys had brought their guitars and a handful of girls stood in an admiring circle around them as they played and sang Dylan songs. And some of the kids just wandered aimlessly around the fire as if mesmerized. As I sat on a huge boulder on the periphery, I felt I was observing a tribal gathering of some primitive culture; and perhaps I was. I would have to remember to tell Travis that, I thought. That was much more something he would say rather than me.

After two Tall Boys I was beginning to feel a little light-headed. I had only drunk one beer on a few occasions before, so I made note to stop at two.

As I was watching the fire send trailers of red streamers into the night sky, I felt an arm slide inside mine.

"Come on, handsome, let's go for a walk."

It was Linda and she led me by the arm into the darkness away from the fire.

"Where are we going? I can't see a thing."

"Trust me," she said. "Just follow me."

As we continued into the night my eyes began to adjust to the darkness, and I felt less like I had to rely on the flawed bat sonar of my youth. We neared a cluster of big boulders, and with Linda still in the lead, we were soon scaling the face of a steep, finely honed, sandstone surface.

"Careful when we get to the top," she said. "Don't overshoot the mark."

Just then Linda disappeared into the night.

"Where the hell are you?" I asked into the darkness.

"Down here," she said as she reached up and grasped my ankle.

"Take my hand and I'll lead you down."

Soon I was by her side on a flat stone shelf, overlooking a glassy reflection of the night sky.

"What the heck is this?" I asked.

"It's a retention pond. Can't you see?"

"No, as a matter of fact, I can't see. I can hardly see a friggin thing," I replied.

Just as I was about to continue, I felt Linda turn, and suddenly she leaned in and gave me a deep, warm kiss.

"Close your eyes," she said.

"Why?" I asked. "It's not like I can see anything."

"It doesn't matter. Close your eyes and promise not to open them until I say it's okay."

"Alright," I said. "They're closed."

"Okay, now don't peek."

"Peek at what, it's totally black out here."

And then suddenly I heard a splash and the ripple of parting water.

"You can look now," I heard from the darkness.

As I opened my eyes, I could make out a rumpled pile of clothes beside me and the night sky was now jumbled and wavy on the surface of the pond.

"Come on in," Linda said from the water, and as quickly as she said it I shed my clothes and jumped headlong into the black.

I felt the cool envelop my body as I sank deep . . . and then I broke the surface with a shout.

"Damn, that water is cold," I said.

Nothing

"Where are you?" I continued.

Nothing

"Linda, where are you?"

And then I felt her smooth body scale my back as if she were a water lizard. As I turned to face her she was gone again.

"I think I'm getting a stomach cramp," I said. "I'd better get out."

Then I hovered silently in the deep water.

After what seemed like a few minutes, I heard a voice out of the darkness.

"Lewis Ray?" she said softly. "Are you okay?"

Nothing

"Lewis Ray. Are you alright?" Now with a little more concern.

Nothing

"Lewis Ray, where are you?"

I could feel the current move as she neared me and I silently treaded water until she got close enough. I bounded into the unknown and grabbed her as she swam by. She let out a scream and just as I was about to pull her to me, she dove for the bottom.

I heard her resurface on the other side of the pond.

"Stomach cramp?" she said. "And I almost fell for it."

Just as I was about to swim toward her voice, I felt the waters move and sensed she was swimming toward me. As I started in her direction, she swam into my arms. Again, her mouth covered mine, and as we kissed, our nude bodies touched at the most sensitive of places. Just as I was about to pull her closer, she was gone yet again.

"You stay in there til I get my clothes on," she said from the ledge. "And don't look."

"Look at what?" I said. "It's still pitch black out here if you haven't noticed."

I heard her giggle as she climbed up the rock.

"Okay, you can get out now," she said. "I'm going on back to the fire. You can find your way." And with that, her profile disappeared over the precipice.

I sat buck naked on the side of the pond, waiting for the night air to dry me before putting on my clothes. Me and Travis are going to have to go to the rock tonight, I thought, cause he ain't going to believe this.

When I got back to the fire Linda was nowhere to be found and Travis was singing a Byrds tune while Johnny Frank strummed along on the guitar. As usual, the crowd was captivated. After a couple of songs, Travis motioned for me to meet him by the car.

"What is it buddy?" I said, sensing some urgency in his demeanor.

"We need to leave," Travis said flatly.

"Okay, but give me just a minute. I need to find Linda."

"We need to leave now, Lewis Ray, and besides, I saw Linda and some other girls leave with Tommy Barker a few minutes ago."

"Okay, but what's the rush?" I said.

"I think I may puke," said a somber Travis.

"Well, go right over there behind that big rock and puke, cause you're not going to throw up in my car. No vomit in the Comet."

"Hell man, I can't puke here. What would people think?"

"I love you, Travis. You're my best friend, and I'll do anything for you, but you're not puking in my car."

"Okay. Let's walk away from the crowd and let me get some air."

After a bit of walking and some night air Travis seemed to feel somewhat better, and when we got back to the fire the gathering was breaking up. On the way home Travis hung his head out the window for a while, much like a Walker Coonhound might, and eventually he lay back and fell asleep.

"Lewis Ray?" Travis said, opening one eye.

"Yeah, buddy."

"You know what you said back there. Did you mean it?"

"I have no idea what you're talking about."

"You said you love me and I'm your best friend. Did you mean it?" Travis asked.

"I don't think I said it and if I did I didn't mean it. You're a dickhead. A drunk dickhead and my best friend is Romey Nobel," I said.

"You just like Romey cause you all get together and masticate," Travis said.

"At least he wouldn't puke in my car."

"I love you too buddy."

"Whatever," I said, smiling into the darkness.

CHAPTER FIVE

Linda's behavior at the swimming hole on the first night we were together would come to be her trademark. Just as she swam into my open arms only to slither away in the black water, she would come to weave in and out of my life, sometimes bringing comfort and excitement, and sometimes wreaking havoc. Somewhat to my surprise, I did lose my virginity to her that summer. Not at all how I had hoped or envisioned, but rather clumsily and awkwardly in the back seat of the Comet on a rainy July night in the parking lot of the Stone Coal Elementary School. When it was over Linda pulled her clothes back on and said she was hungry, so we drove over to the Dixie Drive-In. We ate in silence as the rain droned on the car roof and splattered on the windshield. When we were finished, I sat our tray on the speaker stand and then drove her home.

✳ ✳ ✳

It was in August when I first met Paul Jenkins. Ed had moved out midsummer. He and Mamma had "grown apart" as Mamma explained, but Annie and I were surprised it had lasted as long as it had. Ed was no match for Mamma Lou, but few people were. He was back living with his mother and Mamma seemed to be holding up quite well.

It was a sultry afternoon and I was lying on the couch in the front room in my boxer shorts with the floor fan directed squarely on me. Annie was on the back porch fanning and reading a magazine.

"Lewis Ray," Annie yelled from the porch, "someone's at the door."

I was oblivious to the rapping at the screen door; the fan was humming and I was in that in-between state, not asleep nor awake.

"Get the door Lewis Ray."

Stumbling to my feet, I pulled on my cutoff jeans as I opened the screen.

"Is Lou Slone at home?" he asked.

"It hasn't been Lou Slone in many years and she's not at home. Who wants to know?"

He was dark-haired, taller and thinner than I, and probably a year or so older. By most accounts he would probably be considered handsome. There was a curious charge to our encounter.

"I'm working for the census bureau and I was hoping to catch her at home."

"Well, there's not a whole lot of chance of that happening, so you might as well be on your way." I began to close the screen.

"What's your name?" The census taker asked.

"I'm not in the notion of talking to a head counter. You can come back another time and maybe you'll catch Mamma Lou at home."

"Is that what you call her, Mamma Lou? And you are Lewis Ray." Not so much a question as a statement.

There was an edgy silence between us. He looked at me, and I returned the gaze. Not malevolent, but not warm either.

"I was just going from old records," he continued. "And you have a sister, Anna Reed Jacobs."

"Annie," I said. "And do census takers have names?"

"Yes," he said with an easy laugh. "Paul, Paul Jenkins."

"And where might Paul Jenkins be from? I know most everybody in Pratt County. Who are your folks?"

"Oh, I'm not from around here. My people are from eastern Virginia. I'm just here taking the census to make a few extra dollars over the summer. I sure was hoping to see Lou Jacobs. When might she be home?"

"It ain't been Lou Jacobs for many years either, and your guess is as good as mine as to when she might be home. Keeping up with Mamma Lou is like trying to nail snot to a fence post."

"How long have you lived here in Stone Coal?"

"Do census takers need to know that?"

"No, I'm just curious. I like to get to know the people I meet. That's the best part of this job. Everybody's got a story to tell."

"Well, my story won't fill up a half page in a Blue Horse note-book. I was born here in Stone Coal, have lived seventeen years here in Stone Coal, and will probably die and be buried right here in Stone Coal, more's the pity. How about you, Paul Jenkins, census taker? What's your story?"

"Well, like you, I was born in a small town. My mother and father split up when I was very young. We moved around a lot, mostly East Kentucky and Virginia. I'm soon to be twenty years old. So you can see, my story is about as plain as a brown paper poke. Maybe that's why I like to hear other people's stories so much."

"I hate to break it to you, Paul, but you drove your ducks to a bad pond this time."

"What about your Mamma Lou? What's her story?"

"There's not enough hours in the day nor do you have lines enough in your notebook for Mamma's story," I said, trailing off. "You probably don't want to know anyway."

"I don't have a car here," Paul said. "I took the bus over from Paintsville. Would you give me a ride back to Stone Coal? I would really appreciate it. I walked down here from town, and in this heat it would really be good if I didn't have to walk back."

"Where are you staying?"

"I'm renting a room from a Mr. Bolen, I think his name is."

"That would be Vernon Bolen. He and Helen rent out rooms. That's the closest thing you'll find to a motel in Stone Coal. Let me put a shirt on and I'll give you a ride."

We rode in silence, windows down, with Paul's long dark hair blowing in the wind. It was only a couple of minutes by car, but a long walk on a hot August afternoon.

"Is there a decent place around here to get a bite to eat? I'll buy you a sandwich for your trouble."

"Decent or not, there's only one place open in Stone Coal and that's the Blue Star, Dakey Reynold's place. Dakey sells burgers and bootleg beer. Thelma closes the Whip 'n Sip for a couple of weeks each August and goes to visit her sister in Aberdeen, Ohio. The best place is over in Mill Creek, Dixie's, but I don't want to drive that far. Matter of fact, that's where I work, and I don't really want to go over there on my day off."

"Well, the Blue Star it is. Can I buy you something to eat?"

It was just past three o'clock as we entered the Blue Star, and no one was there but Gay Ramey, the afternoon waitress and cook. Paul and I each pulled up a stool at the counter as opposed to taking a booth, figuring it might be a bit cooler. The big floor fan that stood in the corner slowly turned from right to left and then back right.

"What'll it be guys?" Gay didn't get up from her seat behind the counter. "I've turned the grill and the deep fryer off cause it's so damned hot in here, but I can fix you a cold sandwich and a bag of chips."

"That'll be good," Paul said. "I'll have a bologna and cheese sandwich, a bag of barbeque chips, and a cold Pepsi. How about you, Lewis?"

"Sounds good to me, and it's Lewis Ray or Ray. I don't know why or how, but Lewis just never fit."

"Alright, Lewis Ray then."

"Lettuce, tomato, and mayo?" Gay called over her shoulder as she headed for the kitchen.

"Make mine Miracle Whip and mustard," I said.

Paul and I ate our sandwiches in a comfortable silence, only occasionally commenting on the heat or the lack of anything to do in Stone Coal on a hot August night. After we finished and Paul had paid our bill, I dropped him off at the Bolens' before heading back to the trailer.

"When might we get together again, Lewis Ray?" Paul leaned in the open window.

"Well, if me and my friend Travis get into anything later we'll come by and pick you up."

"Since I don't have a car or anything else to do, I imagine I'll be right here. Thanks for the lift."

"No problem, thanks for the lunch."

About four hours later Travis and I were back in front of Vernon Bolen's house. School was to start back in a few weeks, so we were hoping to have at least one more carefree Saturday night before starting our senior year. And besides, seldom was there a new face in Stone Coal, so it was with intrigue that Travis suggested we invite Paul to go along with us.

"So this guy is a census taker?" Travis looked toward Vernon's house.

"That's what he claimed."

"Huh. Kind of strange, don't you think? The only census takers I have ever known have been old ladies with bad breath and pencils stuck in their buns. My Aunt Ethel was a census taker."

"I'm just telling you what he said."

I honked the horn and Vernon's wife Helen stuck her head out from behind the screen door.

"Is the census taker home?" shouted Travis.

"Just a minute." Helen disappeared and in a bit Paul Jenkins came bounding down the steps.

"I was hoping you'd come back. Not a lot to do here at the Bolens' house." Paul got in the back seat.

"Hey Paul. This is Travis. We were just heading to get some beer and hang out so we thought we'd see if you'd want to go."

"Hell yeah. Good to meet you, Travis."

"You too man." Travis looked Paul over as if he were studying to buy something. He got a quizzical look on his face.

"You look familiar, Paul. Do I know you?"

"Don't think so. Were you ever around Ashland or Grundy?"

"Not really. Maybe you just remind me of someone. Shit, you look like Lewis Ray here!"

"Well I don't see that," I remarked

"Maybe a little," Paul said. "So what do you guys do on a Saturday night here in Stone Coal?"

"Sometimes we go down to Frank Click's hog lot and screw pigs," Travis deadpanned.

"Don't mind him," I said, "he ain't right. Usually we just get a few beers from the bootlegger and go up on the High Rocks and drink. Or we could go to the drive-in movie over at Bosco," I said as I pulled out from the Bolens' drive.

"Sounds familiar," Paul said.

The next stop was at the Blue Star. We had pooled our money and had enough for nine Tall Boys, three apiece. As the sun set over the mountains we found ourselves on the High Rocks looking out over Stone Coal. I wondered how Paul would fit in to the routine Travis and I had established over the years. Travis was the leader, no doubt, but Paul's manner sort of reminded me of Travis's take-charge style. In the few hours that I had known Paul, I had noticed that he asked the questions and led the conversation much as Travis did. This could be interesting. . . . But Paul will be gone in a couple of days and life will be back to the same old boring routine. Or so I thought.

"Tell me about yourself, Travis." Paul took a long pull from his Schlitz.

"Not much to tell. How about you?"

"I've already told Lewis Ray all there is to know about me."

"Well I ain't Lewis Ray."

"So you're not," Paul acknowledged and continued.

"I was raised mostly in Grundy, Virginia. Went to school there. Graduated high school two years back. I work odd jobs and temporary just to get by. Got in a little trouble with the law. They aren't too understanding about protesting strip mines in Buchanan County. That's just about it."

"What is your draft status?" Travis asked. "How have you avoided Nam? Lots of boys older than us have been called up."

"Good as gold. I've got flat feet, a heart murmur, and my dad ran over my foot when I was a kid. They ended up cutting off my right big toe."

"Now that's got to be a good story," Travis said.

"Sometime. Maybe sometime."

"Don't guess you can kill gooks with only one big toe," I interjected with a laugh. What kind of trouble did you get into? Are you a dope-smokin', free-lovin' hippie?"

"Not hardly, just trying to take a stand."

"Hey, I gotta idea." Travis perked up.

"This is never good," I said.

"How so?" Paul asked.

"You'll see."

"No, guys. Hear me out. The Holy Rollers are meeting tonight down at the Phillips 66. Let's go watch. Hell, I may even join up as long as I don't have to wash no feet nor handle any snakes." Travis never lacked for an idea.

The Holy Rollers, formally known as the East Kentucky Holiness Church of Jesus Christ, were a loose-knit group of believers who didn't own a church building, but traveled from community to community on Saturday nights, meeting in schoolhouses or on store porches to spread their particular brand of the gospel. One of the faithful would usually place some flyers on telephone poles and in store windows a few days before the service to generate local interest.

And then the brethren, and I assume sisteren, would show up on Saturday night with guitars, tambourines, hand drums, and a curious black wooden box supposedly full of copperheads and timber rattlers. It was not at every meeting that the box was opened, but was left up to the direction of the Holy Spirit as to whether the assembly would take up serpents.

There would normally be a couple of dozen church members in attendance, and about as many onlookers. We were accustomed to the Old Regular Baptists who sang the high lonesome a cappella dirges, baptized in the creek, and on occasion washed one another's feet. And also the Missionary Baptists who sang hymns to the plunking of an old upright piano and had a built-in baptistery pool. But the Holy Rollers were . . . well, bizarre and intense to say the least. Not only was there the snake issue, and the guitars and drums, but when the Holy Spirit so moved, they would speak in tongues and go into trances—which amounted to spouting forth gibberish before falling dead to the ground and flailing about like a sunfish on dry land.

"Sounds good to me," Paul responded.

"I don't know." I hesitated, thinking that sitting on the High Rocks and finishing up the Tall Boys might be a better choice.

"Aw, come on. They may bring out the snakes tonight." Only Travis could get excited about venomous pit vipers.

"Snakes?" Paul looked at us quizzically.

"Snakes. Copperheads, rattlers, and water moccasins. Only bite the sinners, so we'd better not stand too close. Lewis Ray here has been fornicating with Linda Hudson this very week, so I'd imagine the Holy Spirit might strike him right on the end of his tallywhacker."

"God Travis, only you could think up such shit," I said.

By the time we arrived at the Phillips 66, a crowd had already gathered. The relative cool of the evening had brought respite to the dog-day heat, and a few of the locals milled about on the outskirts of the circle of folding chairs in the graveled drive just in front of the gas pumps. Several women of the church were seated in one section, and a rather large lady with her hair pulled back tight in a bun was thrashing on the guitar beating out the chords to "I Shall Not Be Moved."

"King Jesus is my Captain," she wailed.

"I shall not be moved," the faithful all responded.

"King Jesus is my Captain," the call and response continued.

"Just like a tree planted by the water," the big lady sang.

"We shall not be moved," Travis shouted above the crowd.

"Good lord, shut up," I scolded, as Paul stifled a laugh.

More singing followed, accompanied by banging tambourines and out-of-tune guitars.

"Brothers and sisters come near and let us go to the Lord in prayer."

It was a gnarled little balding man in overalls and a long-sleeved flannel shirt. How in the world he could stand that flannel in this heat was beyond me. Many of the men knelt in the gravel beside their folding chairs. The praying brother began asking God's blessings on all those gathered, both the saved believers, and the sinners—who without redemption would never know the glory of God's heaven but would be left to wither and burn in the lake of fire and brimstone for eternity. As the prayer continued, the fervor and pitch heightened and the believers began shouting affirmations of "Amen" and "Yes Lord." And just as the little gnarly man raised his arms above his head and began to shout to the Lord, wads of white spittle wisping forth with every consonant, Travis joined in the prayer.

"Holy shit, they're going to kill us," I whispered to Paul.

"Yes sweet Jeh-eesus!" Travis shouted.

A few of the faithful began to look sideways from their kneeled positions, sensing this new voice in the cacophony.

"Hallelujah precious Lord!"

If Travis were to be killed this very night, it was not to be my turn as well, so I nudged Paul to the outer edge of the circle.

As the prayer ebbed some in its intensity, as is the natural flow of such a rite, Travis sidled toward Paul and me.

"Don't say another word," I admonished.

"I can't help it if I was slain in the spirit."

"We're going to be slain alright, but not necessarily in the spirit, if you don't quiet down."

Paul was taking it all in. As we huddled at the outermost perimeter of the assembly, a little man, who for all the world looked like a clone of the first little man save for a fringe of graying hair and a white shirt buttoned to the top, began the sermon for the night. He went through the pleasantries of welcoming those members present and extended a special welcome to the guests in their midst. He went on to say that he hoped all in attendance were there to be witness to the incredible power of the Holy Ghost and that if anyone was there as a gawker or to poke fun that they would take their leave now. I suddenly felt as if the eyes of the entire crowd were fixed upon the three of us. When I dared glance upward, I caught Travis out of the corner of my eye nodding affirmations as the strange little man continued.

"The sacraments that we're going to carry out here tonight will be led by the Spirit in response to the call and will of the Lord Jesus Christ, and any blasphemers in our midst should be wary, for God knows the heart of an evil man and His wrath knows no mercy. The Bible says when old Lot left Sodom and Gomorrah, his lustful wife, giving in to the desires of the flesh, looked back for one last glimpse at the cities of iniquities, and God turned her into a pillar of salt. So I'm telling you now, God has warned you through His holy word, if you have an unpure heart and you are here for any reason that doesn't sanctify the name of Jesus, leave now and don't look back."

"I think that's our cue," I whispered to Travis.

"Not a chance," he said with a gritty grin.

"Paul?" I glanced sideways.

"In for a penny, in for a pound." Paul shrugged, palms turned upward.

Once again, I had that familiar feeling of being pulled into something I knew had the potential for a bad end, but just like grabbing old Jonathan's dead hand, I couldn't turn back now.

The preacher continued in his diatribe, rising and ebbing and rising again, each crescendo increasing two steps in intensity and each retard taking just one step back. Soon he was in a full-fledged rant, waving his bone-thin arms just above his shoulders and walking unsteadily among the assemblage. One by one the fervent believers in the inner circle began rising to their feet, shouting and singing and waving their arms toward the sky. The big lady with the bun was the first to be smitten by the spirit and to fall into a holy trance. She started jumping up and down, her ample bosoms bouncing like fishing bobbers on a choppy pond, and her eyes rolled back in her head as she began shouting disjointed words and syllables.

"And the scriptures say some will have the gift of talking in tongues and some shall have the gift of interpretation," the preacher shouted.

Then another of the congregation, an obese middle-aged man in an RC Cola tee shirt, began to speak in the now familiar, unfamiliar tongue, and then another.

"I feel the spirit coming on." It was Travis looking for a reaction.

"Don't you dare."

Even Paul was now looking concerned as he considered Travis joining the litany of jabberwocky.

Before we could think much further, the preacher man in the flannel shirt was in the middle of the gathering holding a worn black wooden box over his head, its size not much larger than a Pepsi case. He shook it violently, invoking the name of the Lord asking that He let His will be known. Some of the believers gathered closer but most of the others moved to expand the circle. The old man then sat the box down in the middle of the congregation and those on their feet who were speaking and interpreting began to dance around the box, inciting an aboriginal feel to the proceedings. Then the old man dropped to his knees and opened the hinged top of the box just enough to insert his thin bony hand. He looked toward the darkening dusk sky and began to recite:

"And these signs shall follow them that believe; In my name shall they cast out devils; they shall speak with new tongues; They shall take up serpents; and if they drink any deadly thing, it shall not hurt them; they shall lay hands on the sick, and they shall recover."

The old man then withdrew his hand from the box and held it high for all to see. With assistance from the others, he arose from his kneeling position and worked his way around the circle with his hand outstretched offering it up for inspection, as testimony that no harm had come to him.

And then the guitar-playing sister with the bun followed suit, and then the man in the RC shirt, and then another, all sliding their hands inside the box and after a time withdrawing them and beholding the lack of injury.

"I could put my hand in there as well," Travis scoffed.

"You could, but you ain't gonna," I stated firmly.

"But I could, cause there's nothing in that box but a handful of creek gravel. Maybe a few chunks of red dog."

Just as the crowd was about to lose interest, a middle-aged man in a work shirt, with the name Melvin embroidered over one breast pocket and Jones Brothers Welding over the other, stepped to the center of the circle. He slipped his hand inside the box and immediately withdrew a rather large timber rattler, its buttons buzzing wildly as the man held the snake firmly above his head, for all to see.

"Holy shit," Travis drawled, sucking in his breath and thinking, I'm sure, that he was glad he didn't succumb to his instinct to expose what he thought to be a hoax.

And then the little preacher in the flannel shirt reached in his hand and withdrew a smaller brownish snake, a copperhead. Two others followed suit. Now there were four snakes being wielded about the crowd, the density of which had sprawled considerably since the introduction of the vipers. In the shuffling that ensued, I ended up across the circle from Travis and Paul. I kept their location in my periphery, while never losing sight of where all four snakes were as well. Those who had taken up serpents all held their snakes in the same manner, grasping firmly about halfway down their length, allowing their reptilian heads to turn and weave, recoil and extend, and their pronged tongues to dart in and out menacingly. The snake bearers danced and sang and chanted as they wove in and out of the crowd, the convicted believers standing their ground and those of little faith providing a wide berth for the procession.

Out of the corner of my eye I sensed new movement on the far side of the circle and I became uneasy, considering that I had not maintained the vigilance of Travis that I normally would under such circumstances. I scanned the arc of onlookers and immediately found Paul, who was nearly a head taller than those about him, but saw no sign of Travis. As the procession of the four snakes moved away from me and toward Paul, the crowd around him thinned in response. I was about to change my vantage point when I saw Travis step out from behind the gas pump. He was crouched over as if he were stalking prey, and in his hand he had a big loop of the air hose. I was hoping against hope that Travis was not about to do that which I felt certain he was intent on doing. And sure enough, just as the snake handlers neared Paul, Travis took the circle of hose and from behind looped it over Paul's head, leaving it to rest on his shoulders and droop toward his waist.

Paul let out a shriek that rang loud above the din and he began to scramble backwards until he tripped and fell over the gas pump island, spilling the water can held there on reserve for overheating radiators. Travis was laughing hysterically.

In the few seconds that followed, events unfolded in an unthinkable and rapid succession. Paul's violent reaction resulted in a confused response from the assembly. Most had no idea what had transpired and were as perplexed by Paul's outcry of panic as by Travis's howling laughter. The little preacher, copperhead in hand, heard the ruckus and pivoted to face the commotion, and as fate would have it, at that very instant Travis bolted upright from his crouched position. Just as Travis stood erect, the copperhead pulled tight, making a compact S against the preacher's knotty fist, then at deadly speed flung itself out, reaching its full extent and sinking its exposed fangs into Travis's left cheek.

CHAPTER SIX

By the time we reached Our Lady of the Way Catholic Hospital in Martin, Travis was barely conscious. He had started talking out of his head a few miles back, his left eye was now swollen shut, and the two puncture marks from the snakebite centered on his left cheek were circumscribed by alternating concentric circles of red and purple.

The scene at the gas station became total mayhem after Travis was bitten. The snake recoiled as quickly as it had struck, and the old man threw it to the ground where it commenced a hasty retreat. As the copperhead slithered through the gravel the crowd began to part, people pushing one another out of the way to escape the confused and angry serpent. Women screamed and men shouted as the snake tried unsuccessfully to coil and strike again, until the man in the RC tee shirt calmly and firmly placed the heel of his brogan on the snake's head and with a few twisting and grinding movements made impotent any lingering danger.

Travis fell to the ground as soon as he was bitten and held his cheek and jaw with both hands, pushing inward with all the pressure he could muster.

"Travis! We've got to get you some help." I was now straddling his supine form, bending to get him to his feet.

"Blasphemers!" shouted the old man who had been holding the now-dead snake. "Blasphemers! God has seen the unrighteous and has smitten them with his mighty wrath. Blasphemers! The lot of you be damned." He was now squarely in my face, shouting, with his specks of spittle spraying me in the eyes.

"Old man if you don't get out of my way, I swear to God I'm going to kick the living shit out of you." I had gotten Travis to his feet, and Paul, who had appeared from somewhere, was now pushing back the advancing pack of onlookers.

"You fellers better get him to the hospital," said a bystander.

"I know, I know. Just clear me a way."

Paul took the lead and cleared a path through the gawkers as I put Travis's right arm around my shoulder, bearing the majority of his weight, and led him to the car.

"Do you know how to drive, Paul?" I asked.

"Sure. Why?"

"I'm going to take care of Travis and you just follow Route 80 west til we get to Martin."

As the onlookers gathered around the car, peering in the windows like turkey vultures over a decaying carcass, Paul pulled out of the gravel drive with me in the back seat, Travis's head cradled in my lap.

"Man, I fucked up this time," Travis said through clenched teeth.

"You're going to be alright. We're just going to get you to Lady of the Way where they'll know what to do."

"Yes, they'll know. Just take care of me, man."

"You got it. Just hang with me."

When we arrived at the hospital, a small two-story building in the center of the tiny burg of Martin, it was nearing midnight. The door marked Emergency Room was locked and a sign over a push button instructed those needing treatment to Ring Bell for Service. Travis's breathing was rapid, and shallow, and I stayed behind with him in the car as Paul rang the bell and waited. At last, after what seemed to be an eternity, a small figure appeared at the far end of the long, brightly lit hall. As it came nearer, I could make out a slightly built nurse in a nun's habit marching toward the plate glass door, a chain attached to a ring of keys dangling from her pocket and swaying in cadence with her quick steps. She opened the door and she and Paul had a brief exchange. The nurse quickly turned and struck a red knob on the wall, which I imagined was a means to summon more help. She then grabbed a narrow gurney and she and Paul rolled it down the ramp toward the car. The three of us hoisted Travis, who was now unconscious, onto the stretcher, his arms and legs flaccid and splayed out. As we rolled through the door, the nun directed Paul and me to a row of metal folding chairs lined down a small corridor off of the main hallway. As she maneuvered the stretcher through double doors she was met by another white-clad nun and a man in blue scrubs, whom I hoped was the doctor. They disappeared and the big doors closed behind them. It was only then that I allowed myself to consider the full potential and impact of the situation. I asked Paul to keep vigil by the double doors. Then I walked out the plate glass entry, down the ramp, through the parking lot, and I sat down on a curb under a dimly lit street light, and for the first time since I was probably seven years old, I wept.

✳ ✳ ✳

Gracie brought us both ice tea in the same tall glasses I remembered from my childhood, flared at the top with daisies painted on them. I was sure they had once contained Bama Apple Jelly.

"I thought it'd be cooler out here." Gracie sat down in a metal lawn chair, another relic from my childhood, and started a familiar bounce as she leaned to and fro.

"Tell me what all has happened to you. Lord, it has been years and years since we've talked."

"Not a lot has happened, Gracie, in some respects, but in others a whole lifetime has passed since I left Stone Coal."

"Didn't you go to the service?"

"Yeah, I did a hitch in Nam. You know Travis and me always said if one of us got called up the other would volunteer. Obviously that couldn't happen. I don't think I've ever been so lonesome in my life as the morning Travis took me to Ashland to the induction center. It was a May morning, way before daylight when we left. I didn't think I'd ever see Stone Coal again."

"Well, was it as bad over there as everybody said it was?"

"Not for me. I lucked out and got assigned to a supply unit. I was pretty much away from any combat. I spent two years ordering and stocking noncombat supplies: canned hams, cigarettes, fatigues, boots, basically anything except weapons or ordnance. Of course we had a lot of guys coming through that were pretty messed up. It was a bad time. It was a bad time for a lot of reasons."

"You know Johnny Frank was killed over there, and Ronnie Hall too. There was a lot more, but them was the only two I knew well. They were regulars at the restaurant when they were coming up."

"Yes, it was bad business. I felt insulated from the real danger, even guilty for my good fortune when I would see those long thin metal coffins being shipped back home. I saw a lot of boys messed up pretty bad, and not just physically."

"You are a good boy, Lewis Ray, or a good man I should say. You'll always be a boy to me. You know, I worried about you back then. I worried that you let Travis do your living. It was hard not to. He cast a big shadow. Everybody adored Travis. He was easy to love, and he was anybody's buddy. But there was something extra between you two that few people shared. He was the more outgoing one, but there was something real about you that ran deep. I always knew how good and how real you were."

"I don't know about that, Gracie. You know, sometimes I think the happiest days of my life were spent right there in that little aluminum house trailer over on Stone Coal, with Annie in the next room and Mamma Lou out ripping and tearing and me and Travis getting into who knows what. But I guess we remember what we want to remember, or remember it how we want to. If those truly were the happiest days of my life I don't guess I'd have dreaded coming back so bad. Naturally, the circumstances today aren't what anybody would look forward to, but it goes deeper than that. It's funny how one thing can happen and in an instant change a whole lifetime. Travis was never the same after that night. In a lot of ways, I wasn't either. I spent years thinking that maybe I could have or should have done something that would have made that night not happen. I finally had to give that up."

"Sometimes it takes getting away from something to really know it, I suppose." Gracie tucked a stray wisp of gray hair back into her twisted bun.

"You are a wise soul, Gracie. You had such a big heart when we were growing up and that's why so many of us flocked to you. You never asked anything of any of us, but expected something good from all of us."

"Well I hate to say it, but you never had much to look up to. Lou probably had more on her plate than she could say grace over, but that was of her own doing. Her younguns just got the leftovers." Gracie continued after a long pause, "I'm sorry, I ain't got no right to talk that way, especially today. But I never understood why women had children and then never paid 'em any attention, when there were women like me who'd have given all they had to be able to have babies."

"But Gracie, you had lots of children. Maybe that was the way it was supposed to be. You were the closest thing to a mother several of us ever knew."

"You know how to make an old woman feel good, Lewis Ray. And what about Paul? Whatever happened to him?"

"Oh, Gracie, I don't even know where to start. With Mamma Lou you never knew what was around the next corner, but Paul was a blindside like I had never experienced before. And having lived with Mamma Lou . . . that's saying a lot."

✳ ✳ ✳

I had walked around Martin for at least an hour before I returned to the hospital. I was afraid to go back and afraid not to. Finally, about three o'clock in the morning, I found myself tapping on the plate glass door to the emergency room. Paul let me in, his eyes swollen from sleep, or a lack thereof, I couldn't tell which.

"Any news?" I asked.

"No, the nurse came out about an hour ago and said he was stable for now and that the doctor was still with him. She said she would let us know as soon as there was anything to tell."

"Paul, this is so unlike me, and so like Travis, but we have a few hot beers left in the car. Let's go out in the parking lot and finish them off."

About five hours later Paul and I were jarred awake by the little nurse rapping her jangling keys against the car window. The sun was streaming bright through the windshield and the floor of the Comet was littered with empty beer cans.

"The doctor wants to see you now. Follow me."

Paul and I tumbled out of opposite sides of the car and followed the sister as instructed, no one speaking. Once inside the plate glass door, which was now unlocked, we followed her through the double doors where Travis had disappeared earlier, then down another narrow corridor and into a small office. Behind a cluttered desk sat a slight little man, not much bigger than the nun who had been leading us. He had on a white lab coat and half-glasses with tortoiseshell frames, the latter of which had probably been purchased from the Ben Franklin five and dime next door to the hospital. He had thin salt-and-pepper hair worn in a crew cut. I supposed this had been his custom since his military days.

"Have a seat boys," the little man instructed, as he waved us toward a couple of metal folding chairs that were identical to the ones we had been shown to by the nun last night.

"I'm Dr. Mason. Who are you?"

"I'm Lewis Ray Jacobs and this is Paul Jenkins and," I began.

"I'm not asking your names. I need to know who the hell you are. Are you brothers of Travis's?" Dr. Mason interrupted.

"No, just friends."

"Well, we have a very sick young man on our hands and I need to talk to his family. He does have family? A father or mother?"

"Well," I answered, "Travis's father was killed several years ago and his mother doesn't do well."

"What do you mean, doesn't do well?"

"She has problems getting out and being around people."

"You mean she has emotional problems," the doctor said, adding clarification.

"Yes sir."

"Well, emotional or not, she needs to get down here."

"Travis is going to be okay isn't he?" I asked, starting to feel a little shaky.

"It's according to what you mean by okay. He is probably, let me emphasize *probably*, not going to die, but there are issues we need to talk about."

"What kind of issues?" I asked.

"Okay, let's back up. Start off by telling me what happened. Travis was able to tell me he got bit by a copperhead, which is actually fortunate, if you're going to get bitten by a poisonous snake. A copperhead is one of the few pit vipers that can release its venom incrementally. Its nature is not to kill, but to fend off an attacker by injecting its painful poison. If the first round doesn't do the trick it saves back enough venom for a second or even third strike. It certainly has enough toxin to kill a human, but usually that isn't the case. A timber rattler, on the other hand, bites to kill. It gives its victim a full dose the first time and a second dose is seldom needed. If Travis had been bitten by a rattler we wouldn't be having this conversation."

"We don't need a biology lesson," Paul interjected, "Lewis Ray here just wants to know about his friend."

"Don't be a smart-ass, son." Dr. Mason shot a hard look at Paul.

"This is Lewis Ray's best friend and we're just trying to find out if he's going to be okay. No disrespect intended."

"Be that as it may, don't be a smart-ass. I have been up for over twenty-four hours, thanks to your all's little snake-handling adventure, and I don't really feel like taking any crap."

"Sorry sir."

"So I understand you all were at a Holy Roller snake-handling meeting. That's another detail Travis was able to tell me," Dr. Mason continued.

"Yes sir," I said. "We were rubbernecking, and things got out of hand and Travis got bit."

"Don't you know the Holy Rollers are crazier than bat shit?"

"Yes sir, that's why Travis wanted to go."

For the first time I detected a hint of a smile from Dr. Mason.

"So, what is going to happen to Travis?" I asked.

"I really need to talk to his mother. Can you bring her here to the hospital? I think we can keep him here. I had originally thought we may need to ship him to Lexington, and we may before it's all said and done, but for now I want him to stay here. A lot depends on how much tissue damage has been done. If it were his calf or thigh, I wouldn't be so concerned, but my God, it's his face. And not more than two centimeters from his eye. I feel certain he has lost, or will lose, sight in that eye. I'm just hoping we can mitigate the cosmetic damage by preserving as much viable tissue as possible."

I didn't understand all of the medical jargon that Dr. Mason was throwing around, but I understood enough to know that Travis would never be the same.

A few minutes later, Paul and I were allowed back to see Travis. The top half of his bed was up at a forty-five-degree angle and he lay motionless on a crisp white starched pillowcase. A bandage covered his entire head, save for the tip of his nose, his mouth, and his right eye; a few strands of his blonde hair stuck out from the edges, and circles of pink-tinged drainage bled through over the spot where the snake had struck. I moved to Travis's right side, hoping he would open his eye, and Paul stood quietly at the foot of the bed.

"Hey turd head," I said softly.

Travis halfway opened his exposed eye and tried to focus.

"Holy shit, my head hurts," he said with a thick tongue.

"Yes, the doctor said you would have a pretty good thumper. He also said they had given you some high-powered pain medication, so you'll spend a lot of time here sleeping for the next day or so."

"That doctor is a real comedian ain't he?"

"Oh yeah."

"I don't know what he means, a few days. I don't plan to be here a few days. Where's Paul?"

"I'm here," Paul said from the foot of the bed.

"What do you think of Stone Coal so far? I did my best to make it not boring."

"If you ever come to Grundy I don't know how I'll top this." Paul smiled.

"Travis," I said, changing the tone of the conversation, "I'm going to have to tell your mother. Dr. Mason wants me to bring her here tomorrow. He's off duty til in the morning, but wants to see her first thing."

"Absolutely not," Travis protested. "I'll be out of here in a couple of days and I'll tell her myself what happened, or at least all she needs to know of what happened."

"There's more. Travis, you got bit real close to your eye. You're going to be in here a while, and you know how stories travel in Stone Coal. Your mamma has to be told and the doctor needs to talk to her."

"Well, it can't happen. I need to get home. Mom will see I'm okay and," Travis began to slur, "I can see to the . . ." Travis's uncovered eye closed.

On the way back to Stone Coal I struggled to stay awake. The morning was giving way to noontime and the heavy Eastern Kentucky heat and humidity was setting in.

"Do you want me to drive?" Paul asked.

"No, just keep talking to me. I'll be okay as long as there's not a lull in the conversation. How long are you going to be around these parts, anyway?"

"I don't know, a few weeks probably."

"A few weeks?" I asked, giving Paul a look. "You can census everybody in Stone Coal, Mill Creek and all points in-between in a couple of weeks and have time left over," I said, indicating a level of skepticism.

"Well, I'm in no hurry to move on. I've been thinking about quitting the census job anyway. I'll just wait and see."

"I hope you aren't planning on finding a job around here. You'll be hard-pressed, unless you want to work in the mines."

"No, I've been back to the mine face one time and couldn't get out of there fast enough. Too much like a damp, dark grave. I don't know, I have a little money saved up. Or I may keep with the Census Bureau. We'll see," Paul said, sounding more evasive than unsure.

I dropped Paul at the Bolens' and headed home for some much-needed sleep, dreading the time I would have to face Ada Wicker and try to explain all that had happened in the last day.

CHAPTER SEVEN

I was dead tired from exhaustion. Sleep was an elusive and intermittent visitor that night, but it had been a fitful respite as I replayed the events of the past two days over and over in my dreams. Mamma had come in about three o'clock in the morning. She had heard all the rumors about Travis, over at Cooley's. She sat on the foot of my bed, insisting on hearing the entire story. By the time she'd gone on off to her room I was wide awake, dreading the day that lay ahead of me. How would I approach Ada? What would I say? How would I choose my words? I had always avoided Travis's mom for all the obvious reasons, and some that weren't so obvious. However, I didn't have to worry long. By six o'clock there was a loud pounding on the front door.

"Lewis Ray! Lewis Ray Jacobs! It's Ada Wicker. You come out here right now. I come to see about my boy. Get up and get out here! I need to know what's happened to my youngun."

I made my way to the front of the trailer and opened the door just as Ada had her clenched hand extended above her head, about to begin another barrage of banging. I instinctively ducked and covered my head with my arms.

"I'm not going to hurt you, Lewis Ray. I just come to see about my boy. I hear he is hurt and you carried him to the hospital."

"Yes, Ms. Wicker. I was going to come and tell you what I know, but was waiting for it to get daylight."

"I was trying to wait too, but I couldn't stand not knowing about my baby any longer. I heard he got snakebit."

Ada Wicker looked so small and afraid in the predawn light. Her eyes were dark and almond shaped. Her curly black hair was pulled back in a ponytail, her wiry thin arms folded tight across her chest, and her hands tucked to her ribs. Her movements were quick, and nervous, and her glance darted from place to place as if she were expecting someone or something to appear from the shadows. Her complexion was white as porcelain, not pale and pasty, but milky and unadorned. I hadn't seen Ms. Wicker close up in several years, but I now understood where Travis got his good looks.

"Holy God, what in hell is going on out here?" It was Mamma Lou, stumbling from her bedroom and looking out over my shoulder as Ada stood nervously on the front porch of the trailer.

Just what I needed, I thought, not one, but two crazy women to deal with.

"It's Ada Wicker, Mamma. She came to check on Travis."

"Well, come on in Ada," Mamma invited. "I'll put us on a pot of coffee and we'll see if we can sort all of this out."

"Thank you Miss Jacobs, or whatever your name is now, but I don't think I'll be coming into your house. Let's talk out here. It wouldn't be right for me to come in."

"What do you mean, it wouldn't be right?"

"Well, for one thing, you're pretty much a whore," Ada accused.

"A what?"

"A whore."

"A whore?"

"Yes, a whore."

"Well, I'll be damned." Mamma laughed to herself. "Like you got some room to talk. I hear that you're crazier than a shithouse rat, too, but come on in. I guess this old slut can fix your loony ass a cup of coffee and maybe we can figure out what to do next. Lewis Ray, honey, you go on back to bed. I'll take Ada here down to Martin soon as I can get all my shit in one bag, so to speak. I've just got to have some coffee, take a spit bath, and put on my face."

Ada warily followed Mamma into the kitchen, choosing to stand in the door rather than to sit at the dinette, and I headed back to my bedroom.

Mamma Lou, the enigma. One never knew what to expect from her. But as I lay in my bed and heard the car, carrying those altogether opposite yet equally crazy ladies, pull out of our drive, I was thankful.

Later that afternoon I picked Paul up and we headed to Martin to check on Travis. August was again bearing down on the valley with a vengeance and the air was thick and hazy.

"How did it go with Travis's mom?" Paul questioned.

"Well, believe it or not, Mamma Lou came to the rescue."

"How so?"

"Ms. Wicker was banging on our door at the crack of dawn. Mamma hadn't been home but a few hours and I was out on the porch trying to handle things. Lo and behold, Mamma gets up out of bed and takes charge of the situation."

"You sound surprised," Paul said, lifting an eyebrow.

"You've never met Mamma Lou. Charity ain't exactly her long suit, but she took Ms. Wicker to Martin to the hospital to see Travis. Just about the time I think I have my mother figured out she up and does something totally out of character, sometimes good, often not so good."

"Not so good? What does that mean?"

"It just means that you never know what's next with Mamma Lou. Tell me about your mother. What's she like? I guarantee she can't compare to Mamma Lou."

"Can't say as I know a whole lot about her. She and my dad were never married. When I was very young she took me to my dad's and dropped me off. I visited my mother a few times, especially when things would go south with dad, but for the most part I was raised by my father," Paul said.

"Did your dad ever marry?"

"No. A Mexican woman named Rosita lived with us for several years, but she and dad eventually split up. Never were married as far as I know."

"You have any brothers or sisters?" I asked.

"Boy, you're the one writing the book now. Do you think Mamma Lou and Ms. Wicker will still be at the hospital? I'd like to meet your mother."

"Don't know. I guess we'll see." I pulled into the Our Lady parking.

A large woman wearing a pink bibbed dress and a name tag proclaiming her to be Agnus Sizemore, Ladies Auxiliary Volunteer, looked up from her *Grit* newspaper as we approached the front desk. Travis had been moved to a room on the second floor she told us as she pointed down the hall.

"Take the stairs," she said in a monotone. "Elevator is for patients, staff, and old people, and you are neither."

Down the long shiny hall we passed an older man in blue hospital clothes operating a buffing contraption. We timed our passage so as not to interfere with the side to side sweep of his machine. Travis's room was the last one on the left, and it appeared dark and abandoned. Just beyond the half-drawn curtain, we found what we assumed was Travis balled up in the bed under a white sheet.

I gently patted the area I took to be his rear end, and slowly the form unfurled and rolled toward us, then Travis's bandaged head emerged from the cocoon.

"Hey," was all that I could think to say.

"Hey," Travis said back, with his one exposed eye half-open.

"How are you feeling?" I asked.

"How do you think?" Travis said without emotion.

"Like you've been bit by a copperhead?"

"Not funny," Travis said, turning his face to the wall.

"Sorry." I felt stupid.

Paul remained silent.

"Anything I can do for you?" I asked.

"Yes, leave," Travis said.

"Leave?"

"Yup."

"Why? We just got here."

"Just go. I don't feel like talking." Travis was still turned to the wall.

"We don't have to talk. We can just sit here. Or maybe I can get you something. How about me and Paul go to the Burger Broil and get you something besides hospital food?"

"Please, just go."

"You feeling bad? I can ask Nurse Jolly out there to bring you a pain pill."

"No, just go on home."

"Okay, I'll come back tomorrow."

Travis rolled over to face me. Tears were streaming from his exposed eye.

"Don't come back tomorrow or the day after or the day after that. I don't want company. I just want to be left alone."

"What do you mean? Travis, it's me. It's Lewis Ray. It's your blood brother."

"And I'm one-eyed Travis, a carnival freak. The doctor says I have to go to surgery and they are going to take out what's left of my eye. He says I'll be disfigured from where the venom ate away part of my face. Of course, a skin graft that they will take from my ass will look like a patchwork quilt. Frankenstein. I just want to be left alone. So please just leave and don't come back."

"I'm sorry, I didn't know."

Paul caught my eye and nodded toward the door.

"Travis, you don't have to do this alone. We are all but brothers," I said, aware my voice was starting to break. "Let me be there for you just once in my life, like you've always been there for me."

"This ain't about you." Travis turned away again. "Just go. And please don't come back."

Paul and I rode in silence back to Stone Coal. I couldn't wait to drop him off at the Bolens'. I only wanted to be alone and I got my wish. When I arrived at the trailer no one was home. I sat on the front porch waiting for dusk and the cool of the evening, hoping that time would pass and still the squall within me. As darkness settled over the valley, I went to the rock and lay looking up at the sky, trying to feel as if I were up looking down, but all I could see was a blankness. I felt sadder than I could ever remember feeling in my life.

✳ ✳ ✳

The next few weeks of summer crawled by. I had honored Travis's wishes and hadn't gone back to the hospital. A week after surgery he had been sent home for his mother to care for him and word was he wasn't seeing anybody, or at least a very few. I had asked Mamma Lou to look in on them, but the more predictable Mamma had resurfaced.

"I took her old crazy ass to the hospital and stayed with her all day. All the time her eyeing me like I was some kind of jezebel. The nerve of her looking down her sanctimonious nose at me, and her being crazy as a fiddler's bitch. She didn't have no trouble finding us when she needed somebody to take her to Martin, and she won't have any trouble the next time she needs something," Mamma said dismissively.

"I guess you're right, but I was just hoping you could check on Travis."

"Well check on him yourself. He's at home. I saw your little girlfriend coming out of his house the other day."

"Linda?"

"Yep."

"What was Linda doing there?"

"Well, I'm sure I don't know," Mamma said. "She's your girlfriend."

"She's just a friend, Mamma."

"Honey, I've been to two county fairs and a mule pulling. This ain't my first trip to town. I can tell the minute I see two people together if they have been doin' the dirty, and you and that girl have been at it sure as I'm sitting here."

"God, Mamma, you think you know everything don't you?"

"Be that as it may, am I right or am I right?"

"None of your business. You, of all people, don't have any room to talk."

"You watch your mouth, young man. I ain't beyond smacking the living crap out of you."

"Well, just don't think I'm stupid, Mamma. I know way more than you think I do. Always have. I get sick of you acting like me and Annie don't know shit."

"Lewis Ray Jacobs, I won't tolerate you disrespecting me that way."

"You're a fine one to be talking about respect. I could never disrespect you more than you disrespect yourself, carrying on the way you do." I was surprised by the words that had come out of my mouth and before I could draw another breath, I felt the sting of Mamma Lou's open palm across my face.

"Mamma, don't you ever lay a hand on me like that again," I said between clenched teeth. "You're always talking about respect, well it's time you treat me and Annie with a little respect."

Uncharacteristically, Mamma retreated. She turned and left the kitchen and went into her bedroom as I headed out the back door. I sat on the steps with my head in my hands. I had never crossed Mamma before, and neither had anyone else as far as I knew.

After a few minutes had passed, and sensing that I needed to fix whatever it was that I felt I had broken, I went back into the trailer. I stood in the doorway to Mamma's room. She was lying across the bed, on her back with her face covered by the crook of her right arm.

"I'm sorry, Mamma."

"No, I deserved that," Mamma said, not removing her arm. "I had no right to smack you. You were just telling the truth."

"Are we okay?"

"Yes, baby. We're always okay, Lewis Ray. We're just trying to find our way in this shitty old world."

"Yep," I agreed, "it does feel pretty shitty sometimes."

I often thought Mamma saw the world as she wanted to see it. She created these ideas in her head and could justify most anything as having a reason and a purpose. Maybe that's how she stilled the storms within her.

"Shitty or not," Mamma said as she slowly rose to her feet, "I still ain't going to check on the Wickers. I have no idea why you don't just go down there and check on them yourself, nor why you haven't darkened their doorway since Travis got home, but I suppose you have your reasons. And you know what I said about knowing people? Well, your little girlfriend looked as guilty as a tomcat that had swallowed a goldfinch when I saw her leaving the Wickers' house."

✳ ✳ ✳

Late summer had always borne an air of sadness for me. Carefree days of swimming in the creek and camping on the High Rocks would soon come to an end. I had heard that Travis wasn't coming back to school in the fall, but may get his GED through home study. I hadn't seen him, but rumors were circulating that he seldom got out of the house.

I spent the waning days of summer break either working at the Dixie or aimlessly driving about. Shortly before school was to start, I passed through Stone Coal one afternoon and saw Linda sitting on the curb outside the Blue Star. I immediately swerved and came to a dusty stop in the gravel parking lot.

"Whoa there, cowboy," Linda said as I got out of the Comet.

"Hey. Long time no see."

"Yeah, I've been missing you. Come and sit down," she said, patting the curb beside her.

"What have you been up to? I tried to call you."

"Yeah, Mom said you had called, and I called you back a time or two, but I guess we never connected."

"I guess not. Well, we are connected now, so what shall we do?"

Linda leaned into me and wrapped my arm in both of hers.

"Let's get a couple of burgers and some beers and go up Big Springs and have a picnic at Purty Place."

"That sounds real good to me," I said, feeling like maybe everything was okay between Linda and me after all.

Purty Place, or Pretty Place to be exact, was a secluded pool at the head of Big Springs, a meandering creek that was a tributary of Ball Branch. An old wagon road followed the upstream path, often traversing the creek and sometimes making its route in the stream's bed. Years of wagon, truck, and car travel had rendered the road fairly passable, as long as you knew the deep holes to avoid and the rock shelves to use for traction. The road ended at what had once been a large homestead. All that remained now was a partial stone foundation and a tumbled-down chimney. The land surrounding the house was overgrown and weedy, but one could easily imagine the grandeur of the once-fertile fields and the orchards with fruit-laden trees. A narrow footpath led from the road to the back of the house; then it disappeared into the dense woods only to reemerge at Purty Place, a cool deep mountain pool bordered by a series of huge flat sandstone outcroppings. The virgin trees that enclosed Purty Place created a botanical canopy which opened only at its center to welcome in the sunlight. Glints of silver shimmered off the glassy veneer of the pond and minnows darted just under the surface. Water dogs rested on the submerged shoals that lined the bank's edge and snake doctors hovered over the placid basin like tiny helicopters.

"This has to be the most beautiful place in the whole entire world," Linda said as we spread a worn quilt I had retrieved from the trunk of the Comet.

"Guess that's why they call it Purty Place, don't you think?"

"Smart-ass."

"Better than to be a dumbass," I said, realizing just how stupid that did indeed sound.

"Barf!"

"Okay, not one of my best." I eased myself onto the blanket, beside Linda.

"Do you have a light?" Linda pulled a pack of Winstons from her purse.

"When did you start smoking?"

"I don't know. Do you want one?"

"Sure," I said. I'd only tried my hand at smoking once or twice before.

"I think I have some matches in the car," I said.

"Let me dig around in my purse," Linda said as she went fishing in her handbag, coming up with a Zippo lighter.

"You smoke funny," Linda commented after I had taken a few draws.

"Well, honestly it's not something I have a lot of experience with. What am I doing wrong?"

"First of all, you are blowing smoke out of your nose like a bull getting ready to charge. And you're making a huffing noise. Calm down and enjoy the experience. It's not work."

"Okay." I took a full draw and inhaled deeply. Just as I was about to slowly release a gentle, controlled plume of willowy haze, my body was racked with a convulsive fit of coughing. Smoke and spit exploded from my nose and mouth and my chest burned like a house on fire.

"How was that?" I managed after a few more moments of respiratory stridor.

"Very cool. Do it again."

"I think I'll pass. Maybe smoking is not my thing."

I lay back on the quilt, allowing fresh air to displace the fire in my lungs, and then as I was just about to sit upright again, the world around me began to spin.

"I'm feeling ill," I sheepishly admitted.

"I used to do that too. Take off your shirt."

Too dizzy to question, I slipped my tee shirt over my head and Linda quickly balled it up and dipped it into the cool water of Purty

Place. She then gently and carefully patted my forehead and cheeks, allowing the water to stream back into my hair and down my neck.

"Thanks. Now this is embarrassing."

"Shhhhh . . ." She continued to soothe me and in a few minutes the vertigo began to subside.

When Linda finished tending to my face and neck, she again dipped the shirt into the restorative waters and began her therapy on my bare chest. I sensed a change from healing to sensual in her attentions, and my body responded to her touch accordingly. She moved from my torso to my abdomen, then gracefully slipped her hand beneath the waistband of my Levis.

✳ ✳ ✳

"Well, you've given me a new reason to love Purty Place," I said as we put our clothes back on.

"Do you mind if I smoke?" Linda asked.

"As long as you don't mind if I don't."

"Please don't," Linda said as she pulled another Winston from her purse.

"Have you see Travis in a while?" I had decided beforehand not to initiate this conversation, but it just came out.

"Why do you ask?"

"Just curious," I replied.

"Curiosity killed the cat."

"Don't talk in riddles. I just asked you a question. Have you seen Travis lately?"

"Well don't be so defensive. Yes, I have. I saw him a couple of days ago. Now, why do you ask?"

"Just wondering how he's doing."

"Why don't you go see for yourself?" Linda responded.

"The last time I saw him it didn't go so well," I explained.

"That was in the hospital. He's better now. Just stop in."

"Is that Travis talking or you talking?" I asked.

"Mostly me, I guess. We have talked. He misses you. Your buddy Paul stopped by earlier this week."

"I'm not so sure he's my buddy. I haven't seen him in a couple of weeks either."

"He took an apartment over Willard Terry's hardware store. Says he may stay around here for a while," Linda continued.

"Well it seems like you know about everything," I said with more of an attitude than I had intended to show.

"Why is that a problem?"

I had no answer. I pulled the wet tee shirt on over my head and motioned for us to head back to the car. The sun was setting by the time I pulled into the approach to Linda's house. As the car came to a stop Linda scooted across the seat and gave me a sisterly peck on the cheek.

"Thanks for the day," she said. "Thanks for the burger and the beers and the . . . uh . . . well, thanks."

"When are we going to get together again?"

"I'll see you around." She slid to the passenger side and disappeared into the dusk.

CHAPTER EIGHT

The following Saturday morning I woke early and headed for Stone Coal to Willard Terry's Hardware. The usual crowd of loafers had already begun to gather on the store porch, older men with nothing to do but whittle and gossip. Willard was sweeping the mounds of cedar shavings from the porch into the parking lot as the men, sitting straddle-legged on benches and Pepsi cases, were generating a new day's supply.

"Howdy, Lewis Ray." Willard looked up from his sweeping.

"Morning, Mr. Terry. Is Paul Jenkins in his apartment?"

"Don't really know. You can check. The stairway is to the back of the feed room. It's open. Just go on up."

I entered the cluttered sales floor and wound my way through rolls of tarpaper roofing, kegs of nails, and reels of barbed wire. Behind the counter was a door which opened into a big room that was stacked nearly to the ceiling with sacks of all varieties of livestock feed. At the very back was a small staircase that led to the second floor. I went on up and followed a long windowless hall til I found a door bearing a card with Paul's name inscribed in pencil.

"Hello . . . anyone home?" I pecked on the door.

Paul was quick to answer and invite me in.

"Nice place," I said, looking around.

"Well it ain't the Holiday Inn, but it beats a room at the Bolens'. I've got my privacy here. There's a rear entrance, so I come and go as I please. Only drawback is I always smell like hog feed. The other two apartments are empty now, so it's just me. Not much to do. I've been reading a paperback that someone had left downstairs. What's up?"

I surveyed the sparse room. A two-burner hot plate sat on the Formica counter, in between a one-compartment sink and a collection of canned goods that could give you heartburn just by looking at the labels. A bed, a dresser and nightstand, and little else made up the furnishings.

"Where's the bathroom?" I asked.

"Down the hall. It's unlocked."

"I don't need to go," I said. "I was just wondering."

"Willard has an icebox downstairs in the feed room he lets me use, so I make do."

"I figured your work here would be finished," I said, with a certain amount of skepticism.

"Oh, I quit the census job. I decided to just hang out here for a while."

"I don't know why," I responded. "What are you doing for money?"

"Not enough. Willard lets me deliver and run errands, but he only pays me by the job. Like he'll say, 'Boy, run this load of feed up to Long Fork. I'll give you two dollars when you get back.' I don't think Willard is going to hurt himself by being overstaffed. I have a few dollars saved from the census job, but I can't last long without fairly steady work. I'm supposed to give Willard twenty-five dollars a month for the room, but he's letting me pay by the week. In the one week I've been here I've made just enough to break us even."

"That sounds like Willard. Mamma Lou is buying our trailer from him on a land contract. He knows how to make a penny off a dirt clod."

"Well, I'd offer you a place to sit down, but short of the bed, I'm all out of sitting room." Paul laughed.

"No problem. I've got to be going anyway. I have to work this afternoon at the Dixie. I had heard you were still in Stone Coal, so I just thought I'd see what was going on. Maybe we can get together tonight. I'll come by after work. Say, Linda says you've seen Travis."

"Yeah, I stopped by his house. Why?" Paul responded.

"No reason, just curious. How is he?"

"I don't know. Hard to say. I only met him a few hours before all hell broke loose, but Linda says he's different," Paul continued.

"Linda says? Boy, you and Linda seem to know just about everything."

"Why does that upset you? It's no big deal. I hardly know anyone here and am just trying to keep in touch with the few friends I have met."

"Like you say, it's no big deal. I've just been out of sorts lately, you know, with Travis getting hurt and all. Things just aren't the same. Maybe I'll see you tonight."

✳ ✳ ✳

Work seemed to creep by that afternoon. When I wasn't washing dishes or cooking short orders, Gracie kept me entertained with her stories. Gracie had great stories, and she always started by asking you had she ever told you the one about . . . ? Of course, the polite answer was no, and even if she had it was well worth it to hear it again.

"Lewis Ray, you sure do appear to be down in the mouth today," Gracie observed.

"Yeah, Gracie, I have been going through a rough patch."

"Wouldn't have anything to do with your buddy Travis would it?" Gracie asked.

"Yeah, that and other stuff too. Things just aren't turning out like I thought they would, this being my senior year and all."

"You want to talk about it?" Gracie asked.

"Not really. Not just now. You know what I need the most? I need one of your stories," I said, forcing a smile.

"Did I ever tell you the one about the old woman who came back from the dead?" Gracie started.

"I can't say as you have."

"I've heard all my life that this is true. There was this old woman who was eating a June Apple. They say it was the sourest June Apple ever you could eat. Well just about halfway through her apple, she commences to getting choked. She spits and sputters and gags and coughs, and all of a sudden she sucks a big piece of that apple core down her windpipe and it hangs up tighter than Dick's hatband. The old woman rocks back and forth a few times, and afore long she turns blue as a fishhook and falls over dead as a coffin nail. Well, they have a wake and have the old lady laid out and all the neighbors come in and her poor old man is way past consoling. He cried tears big as horse biscuits for three days. So after the funeral the neighbor men are carrying the woman's coffin up to the family graveyard, and just about the time they get close to the cemetery one of the pallbearers trips and falls. This upends the casket and it takes a tumble and the old woman comes rolling out. She hits the ground so hard that that piece of apple core shoots out of her mouth and she takes in a deep breath and coughs and sputters and lives for fifteen more years. And fifteen years later, the same thing happens. She's eating a June Apple and a piece of core gets hung in her windpipe and she ends up dead again. Well the poor old man is mourning and crying, but when they get up to the gravesite and start to set the casket down the old man says, 'Put her down easy, boys. Remember what happened last time.'"

Gracie cackled, revealing her trademark gold tooth.

"Gracie, you're telling me a big fat lie." I laughed.

"No honey, I swear I heard it to be the truth."

"You and your stories. You're worse than Travis," I said, without thinking.

"Tell me, how is Travis?"

"I haven't seen him since he was in the hospital. I guess he's doing alright."

"I heard that it put his eye out, that snakebite."

"Yes, that's what I heard too," I replied.

"I can't believe you ain't been to see him. You two have always been like butter beans and cornbread, wherever you see one you see the other."

"I don't know, Gracie. I expect Travis is going through a really tough time. He asked me not to come back to see him," I confessed.

"You never know how people are going to bear up under things, do you? Why don't you just go see him anyway? I bet he'll be glad you came."

"Maybe . . . maybe not. I ain't up for finding out just yet," I said.

"I can see that. Why do you think it is he don't want to see you?" Gracie questioned.

"I don't know, Gracie. Why do you think?"

"I have an idea. Of course you probably figured I would, didn't you?" Gracie smiled as she continued. "Travis has always been the fair-haired child, even though he has come up hard, with losing his daddy, and Ada being so quare. But he's never had to work at anything. People, they like Travis. They like being around him. They take a shine to him. He's the life of the party, the one in the center. And now all of a sudden he sees that slipping away. I'm sure he's wondering how he will face people with his disfigurement. He's got to be mad as h-e- double l. I remember when it became clear that I was barren. I had always dreamt of having babies. I wanted to have a houseful. Mean little boys and sweet little girls. I had it all planned out. Well, when it didn't happen I got mad as a wet hen. I was mad at everybody and everything, but Opp was who got the worst of it. I cried to myself, but I lashed out at Opp. I think deep down I knew Opp loved me and he could take my anger. Nobody else could. I wouldn't expect anybody else to. And even though I saw it driving a wedge between us, I couldn't stop myself. It may just be that you're the only person who Travis trusts enough to let all of that mad out on."

"Maybe you're right, Gracie. It will just have to work itself out. And you were right to be mad because you couldn't have babies. You'd of made one hell of a mother."

"You're a good boy, Lewis Ray." Gracie patted the back of my hand.

"Well," she said, standing, "let's get these dishes washed up and the floor swept and mopped so we can close up and get out of here."

I got a bucket of hot water from the mop sink and poured two glugs of Lysol into it. Gracie began scouring the griddle with a pumice grill brick.

"You still seeing that little girl from down below Stone Coal?" Gracie called over her shoulder.

"Gracie, how is it you seem to know everything?"

"I don't know everything, just all that I need to," she said, turning from the grill.

"So, are you?" She did not relent.

"It depends on what you mean by seeing."

"You know exactly what I mean by seeing," Gracie declared.

I wrung the oversized mop out into the bucket and began my cleaning, paying particular attention to the areas of spilled Pepsi and tracked-in mud.

"What you said about me being a good mother," Gracie continued, "well, part of that is telling your younguns when you see them messing up. I ain't your mother, and I ain't saying you're messing up, but just be careful. I know trouble when I see it, and that little girl is trouble."

It was well after dark when I got back to Stone Coal. I noticed Paul's light was on in his room above the hardware store, so I decided to stop in and see if he wanted to go to the Blue Star to hang out for a while. As I parked in the side lot, I noticed that, curiously, Mamma Lou's car was there as well. I made my way to the rear of the building and found the back door to be unlocked. I let myself in, taking care not to be heard, at least not until I could figure out what was going on. What on earth would Mamma Lou be doing at Paul's apartment? She had never even met him, to my knowledge. I felt the usual tightness in my throat and chest that always precedes a Mamma incident. One would think that with Mamma Lou you would come to expect the unexpected. But, such was not the case. Every time it was like a new experience. The only constant was the upset that welled in the pit of my stomach when another of her exploits was about to be played out. This could not be good. It was never good.

I inched across the oiled floor of the feed room and made my way up the first few stairs. I hadn't moved so stealthfully since Travis and I had invaded Jonathan Waddles's wake those many years ago.

I paused to see if I could distinguish any conversation, but muffled voices were all that I could hear. I carefully ascended the remaining steps, and when I reached the top I eased myself to a sitting position on the landing. I could see that Paul's door was open and someone was standing in the entry, casting a long shadow down the hall.

"What do you want from me?" Mamma's voice was shrill.

"I'm not sure. I just thought I needed to meet you."

"Well if it's money, you are shit out of luck. What you see is what you get, a trailer mortgaged to the hilt and a car that barely runs," Mamma continued.

"I don't want money. I just want to come to know Lewis Ray and Annie. After all, I am their brother. Haven't you ever wondered? Didn't you think I may show up one of these days?"

"Honey, this old gal has been too busy raising two children and keeping a roof over our heads and groceries in the Frigidaire to be thinking about anything else. So now that you've come and you've seen, why don't you just bundle your shit up and head back to wherever you came from. And by the way, tell your daddy I said 'Fuck You.'"

"I haven't seen Dad in a while. I guess he's still welding around Ashland, if he's working at all. But if I see him I'll be sure and relay the message."

"Don't be a smart-ass, son."

"What do you expect from me?"

"I expect you to go right back to Ashland and put all this behind you. There's nothing for you here. You've made something up in your mind that's pie in the sky. A big happy family reunion.

Well, it ain't happening. I don't have the time nor the energy for this foolishness. I've had it rough. Damn rough, thanks in large part to your worthless father."

"That's bullshit. Look around you. What makes you think you've got it any worse than anybody else? You have no idea what my life has been like."

"And that's not my problem. You've seen what you came to see, so just leave."

"No! I've got a brother and a sister here who don't even know me. It's taken me twenty years to get here and I'm not going to leave just because you say so. You may not want to have anything to do with me, and that's your business, but what about Lewis Ray and Annie? Don't they deserve to know about me? And don't I deserve a chance at being a part of their lives?"

"Don't you dare go messing in my children's lives. Just get the hell out of here."

"What about my life?" Paul's voice was trembling. "What about my life?"

"Young man, I mean you no harm, but just get your shit and get the fuck out of Stone Coal." Mamma showed not a shred of compassion.

"Not til I know the whole story."

"Okay," Mamma said, "do you really want to know all of this? Be careful what you ask for. You've probably built some storybook tale in your mind, but if you insist, what I'm about to tell you will bust your little bubble like shooting a balloon with a BB gun."

I swallowed back the harsh bile I felt rising in my throat. My hands were shaking and despite my desire to run, I retreated down the steps as quietly as I had ascended them and left the store unnoticed.

I drove around Stone Coal for a time. I slowed by the approach to Travis's house, even stopped on one trip around, but then sped back up. I circled both the Blue Star and the Whip 'n Sip before finally stopping at the pay phone outside the post office. Linda picked up on the third ring.

"Hey Linda, it's me, Lewis Ray."

"Hey," Linda said, "what's happening?"

"I know it's late, but I was wondering if you would like to hang out for a while?"

"It's not like I got anything else to do." Linda laughed.

"I'll pick you up in a few minutes."

"Just give me time to change clothes. I'll meet you down by the road. Don't pull in the drive. No use to stir anything up with my mother."

I stopped by the Blue Star and spent my last five dollars on two half-pints of Kessler, the bootleggers' standard rotgut whiskey. By the time I reached Linda's house I had downed three or four big gulps, and I could already feel the heat radiating from my face.

"Hey, sexy." Linda was waiting when I pulled up.

"Hey yourself." The alcohol had boosted my courage.

"Where do you want to go?" I asked.

"You called me, remember? You pick it." Linda scooted across the seat and ran her hand through my tousled hair.

"You want a drink?" I offered up the bottle.

"Not without a chaser. Stop by the pop machine at the Phillips 66 and I'll get us a couple of Pepsis." Linda was digging in her purse for change.

By the time we arrived at the entrance to the Three-Room Cave it was nearly midnight. The cave had once been a tourist trap used to lure passersby from out on State Route 6. The roadside signage had boasted three large chambers and had billed it as the "Mammoth Cave of the Mountains." Nothing could have been further from the truth, a fact that may have led to the eventual demise of the venue. The Max Cornett family had operated the cave for several years, charging admission and selling refreshments and cedar trinket boxes to tourists, but it had been closed now for over a decade. A chain-link fence had been erected to block the trail leading up to the abandoned attraction and the ticket booth and concession stand had been overtaken by kudzu.

"Follow me," I instructed, as I got a blanket and a flashlight from the trunk. Linda carried the Pepsis, and I had what was left of the Kessler stuck in my two hip pockets. I led the way, shining the flashlight along the perimeter of the fence until we came to the point just beyond the trees where a breach in the chain-link allowed entrance to the trail. We followed the path up the steep incline, and finally arrived at the mouth of the cave.

"This'll do," I said, spreading the blanket just under the overhang that marked the entrance to the first chamber.

"So we're not going into the cave?" Linda asked, seeming somewhat relieved.

"Why? It's not bad if you don't mind a few bats and snakes."

"I'm fine here. Is it really filled with bats and snakes?"

"Not really," I confessed. "It's just damp and stinky. You've never been in there?"

"No, and I don't plan to start now. Anyhow, it's not like you to call and want to go out in the middle of the night. You are acting all different and strange, so what's going on? Are you okay?" Linda scooted closer to my side on the blanket.

"I'll build us a fire." I got up and started combing the area for some dead wood, of which there was plenty. In no time I had a warm, crackling blaze going.

"Come here." Linda patted the blanket beside her.

"What's going on?" she said as I sat down next to her.

"Let's not talk right now," I said. I took another slug from the whiskey bottle and accepted a chaser as Linda handed me the now-warm Pepsi. Putting the bottle aside, I pulled Linda to me and lay back on the blanket. My lips found hers and I kissed her as I had never kissed anyone before. I could feel Linda give in to my advances and I began to wonder whether my newfound confidence was related to the whiskey or if I had just come to the place where I really had nothing left to lose. Always before, Linda had been the aggressor. But now my hands were instinctively drawn to places I had never been before and my every movement felt sensual and with purpose. I don't know if my passion was fueled by desire or anger, or some combination of the two, but Linda melted under my touch and responded as if I were a seasoned lover. She inhaled sharply, then moaned with pleasure. I felt as if a whole new world was opening up to me. Linda seemed to sense this new awakening as well, for her reaction was raw, almost feral, and real. When we were finished I fell back on the blanket, feeling every beat of my rapid pulse pounding throughout my body. I waited for my breath to return to normal. Linda threw a leg and arm over me and as she rested her head on my chest, I pulled her close. As the fire died and the crickets sang their end-of-summer lament, I felt the entire world drift away and for a moment before sleep overtook me, I stared into the starry sky and had the sensation that I was up looking down.

The morning sun burned hot and bright as I emerged from a coma-like sleep. Before opening my eyes, I began to take inventory of the previous night. My first recall was the unbelievable experience of lovemaking, but the memory was soon tainted by a nagging notion that there was more. And then the memory of Mamma and Paul Jenkins and their conversation in the apartment over the hardware store came flooding into my consciousness. I sat up with a start, my head again thumping with every beat of my heart, but this time with a relentless ache that caused me to bury my face in my hands. I slowly opened my eyes and took in my surroundings. Then, I realized I was naked and alone. I pulled the blanket across my lap and located my clothes in a crumpled pile by the cold ashes from last night's fire. Beside me were the empty whiskey and Pepsi bottles. I gathered my clothes and began to dress. I hopped on each foot as I pulled my jeans on, one leg at a time, weaving like a cattail in the wind, and I took a leak before heading to the car. The liquor that had bolstered my courage and confidence last night had left me bleary and unclear this morning.

When I got to the Comet I saw a piece of paper tucked under the windshield wiper, waving in the breeze. *Woke up early and decided to hike to town. LH*

CHAPTER NINE

The beginning of my senior year was nothing like what I had imagined or anticipated for all these years. It was the first first day of school, in my entire life, that I hadn't shared with Travis. I felt as unbalanced as a three-legged goat. Now that I had my car I had imagined that I would swing by Travis's house every morning on the way to school. We would get an early start and stop by the Blue Star for some coffee and a grilled Honey Bun, Dakey's breakfast specialty. We'd take our time getting home every evening, maybe stopping by Joe Kilgore's restaurant. But that wasn't the way it worked out. I had heard that Travis was having a visiting home teacher from the board of education who was to help him get his GED, but this was just rumor. I hadn't gone back to see him since he requested that I not, and the longer it went the more difficult I knew it would be. After the Paul Jenkins incident it seemed all the more urgent on the one hand, but all the more daunting on the other. Paul disappeared from Stone Coal just as he had arrived—abruptly and without explanation.

I wanted to confront Mamma, or Paul, or someone. I wanted to talk to Annie about all of this, but I knew it would upset her. It seemed easier just to let it go, at least for now. Living with Mamma Lou had given me lots of ways to cope, but the mainstay was to hunker down and wait it out. Whatever it was would change. Maybe for better or maybe for worse, but it would change. Still, I had unfinished business that would just have to wait. Until when, I had no idea, but sometime.

"Hey dickwad!"

I felt the sting of a slap on the back of my head. Oh God, it was Johnny Frank, and I'd rather have a toothache than deal with him, especially today.

"Did you ever think we'd be seniors?" Johnny said.

"Pretty amazing," I agreed, especially since I was surprised that Johnny had advanced past the third grade.

"Yep, here we are seniors. As soon as this year's over I'm joining the army. I could already since I'm nineteen, except I ain't got a diploma yet. I bet you miss old Travis don't you? I hear he ain't coming back this year since he got his eye put out. You and him used to be thick as cold peanut butter."

"Yes, we did." I was keeping my responses to a minimum.

"You all 'bout half acted like you were queer for each other."

"Johnny, please quit while you're ahead. Just shut your pie-hole before you take things too far." I turned and walked toward the courtyard in the center quad of the school.

"Well, I don't guess he's queer for you cause I hear he's screwing your little girlfriend," Johnny yelled after me.

I turned, and lowering my head and tucking my chin, ran straight for Johnny Frank. I charged him as a barmy bull would and as my head, firmly set deep into my squared shoulders, connected with his large flabby belly, I heard him heave and felt his body give way. Johnny doubled over and fell to the ground, his mouth gaping like a goldfish dropped on the kitchen counter. He bit at the air, gulping and attempting with all his might to suck oxygen back into his empty lungs.

"You fuck," he silently mouthed, his eyes wide with panic. I jumped astraddle of Johnny's writhing form and drew back my right arm, cocking it like a .45, my fist perfectly formed to deliver a fierce blow, then someone grabbed my forearm from behind and spun me around. I found myself facing Mr. Gordon, the school principal, a rather formidable figure himself. One of the teachers had heard the commotion and was now kneeling at Johnny Frank's side. Just then I heard a loud sucking sound as Johnny's lungs reinflated after what must have seemed like an eternity to him.

"Lewis Ray, report to my office. I'll be there directly," said a stern and unemotional Mr. Gordon.

Johnny Frank and I sat side by side on the wooden bench in the anteroom of Mr. Gordon's office, both looking straight ahead and neither acknowledging the other's presence. Judy Sizemore, the school secretary, was tapping mechanically at the keys of her IBM Selectric typewriter. She did not look up and kept her manuscript hidden by a piece of cardboard taped to the side of her bookcase. Judging by the heightened security, it could be assumed she was typing the mimeograph for an upcoming exam.

Johnny Frank was summoned first, leaving me to stare at my shoes and wait my turn.

"Hear you boys had a little set-to," Judy said, taking a break from her ratta-tap-tap.

"Not much of a one." I sighed.

"Enough of a one to get you a three-day vacation I'll bet." Judy resumed her task.

So on the first day of my senior year of high school I was suspended for the remainder of the week for delivering to Johnny Frank that which most of the school had long wished to, and several had on occasion done. Since Johnny Frank didn't throw a punch, he was remanded to after-school detention for the next three days, the reason being he instigated a confrontation. On that basis, he should probably be in after-school detention in perpetuity, cause anytime he opened his mouth he seemed to offend or generally piss someone off.

I never understood how a respite from school was to be considered a punishment. I guess if your parents were involved it could have repercussions, but I was pretty sure I could pull this off without so much as a notice from Mamma Lou. Given the facts, I had come out pretty well. Much better than Johnny, who had to not only stay in school, but stay there longer each evening. I began thinking of what Travis would do in such a circumstance, and instantly I knew. It was now Tuesday and I was not allowed back on school property until the following Monday. The more I thought about it, the more apparent it became. God, this would be so much better if Travis were with me, and I had a fleeting thought of going to get him, but maybe it was time for me to venture out on my own. I thought of Mamma

Lou's trite old saying, "when God closes a door he opens a window," however, I had a hard time believing any of this was God's doing. I had long since decided God seldom got around to Stone Coal, and when he did he didn't quite make it to our trailer. But I did get great satisfaction in finally giving Johnny Frank his comeuppance.

That evening when I got home from school, I emptied the White Owl cigar box that I kept hidden in the top of my closet. I had a grand total of twenty-eight dollars and ninety-five cents that I had squirreled away, most of it from working at the Dixie.

I spent the evening putting a few things in the trunk of the Comet: canned food, blankets, a flashlight, a few tools, and anything else I thought might come in handy. Mamma wasn't at home, which wasn't unusual. She often didn't come home until the wee hours if at all. Since Annie was now out of high school and I had started my senior year, Mamma said she considered us both adults and would no longer be treating us as children. Neither of us knew exactly what that might look like, for we had never been treated like any other children that we knew, except maybe for Travis.

So early on a September Wednesday morning in 1967 I set out. I scratched out a message on a sheet of notebook paper and left it on the kitchen table. *Going to be gone for a few days. Don't worry. Will explain when I get back. L.R.* That should keep Mamma satisfied and hopefully allay Annie's fears that perhaps I had been snatched by aliens. Although Annie, I'm sure, had heard about the dustup between Johnny Frank and me and would suspect this was somehow connected.

The sun was just starting to peek over the High Rocks as I passed Travis's house. He'd still be sleeping, I thought. So much of me wanted to turn in to his drive and rustle him out of bed.

"Hey dipwad, how about a road trip?" I'd say.

"If you're waiting on me you're backing up." Travis would roll out of bed, pulling his clothes on as he headed out the door.

But that was before we had made the decision to go to the Holy Rollers' snake handling. Everything had changed since then.

At just after eight a.m. I came to the Black Cat in Prestonsburg and officially passed the milestone that marked the furthest I had ever driven from home. I thought about stopping in for a cup of coffee, but I figured I'd better preserve my limited supply of money. I had no idea how much gas I would need nor what expenses I might incur. I had never been on a road trip before.

From Prestonsburg and on to Paintsville, the hills seemed to open up and the narrow valleys of the mountains gave way to the wide river basin of the Big Sandy. The dog days of summer were over and the sky was a deep autumn blue, and a trace of color could already be seen on the tips of the sugar maples. In the fields the corn tassels were brown and the remaining ears drooped from dried stalks like withered limbs from skinny old men.

From Paintsville I knew to head north, but just where north I wasn't sure. Several route signs pointed in all directions from the main intersection at town center, but the numerical references meant nothing to me. For some reason US 23 North sounded like a good route to take, so I did. It was just past noon and I spotted a roadside park, complete with picnic tables and a sign advertising a scenic overlook. Overlooking what I wasn't sure, but it seemed as good a place as any to eat lunch. I parked the Comet and retrieved a can of Vienna Sausage, or vi-eeny as we called it in Stone Coal, a hot Pepsi, and a pack of saltines from my stash in the trunk. Taking a seat on a picnic table, I surveyed the valley below. It was indeed an overlook, but all I saw was a coal-littered railroad track paralleling what I guessed to be the Licking River. Beyond the river lay an open bottom that was already downy green from an emerging field of winter wheat.

"Hey there, do want something better than a can of vi-eeny for lunch?" called a woman from a few tables down, the only other inhabitant of the park.

"Thanks, but I'm okay."

"I'm going to throw a couple of perfectly good fried chicken thighs to the dogs now, so you'd best take advantage," she said, walking toward my table, wax paper-wrapped chicken in hand.

"Well, in that case, don't mind if I do," I said, putting my vi-eeny and crackers back into my parcel for later.

"Lewis Ray Jacobs is my name," I said, accepting the gift, a bit unsure of what etiquette would be called for in such a situation.

"Well Lewis Ray Jacobs, I'm Charlene Devine."

Now that she was closer, I guessed Miss Charlene Devine to be somewhere north of thirty-five years old. Her hair was unnaturally blonde, and her meticulously applied makeup just barely covered a smattering of freckles across the bridge of her nose. She wore a sleeveless yellow summer dress and she smelled of lilac.

"Thank you, Miss Devine, for the lunch."

"Please, Charlene."

"Okay, thank you Charlene."

"Well, you're most welcome Mr. Lewis Ray Jacobs. What is a young, and I might add handsome, fellow like you doing out here on this old lonesome stretch of road on a day like today?" She took a seat on the table beside me.

"Well, I could ask you the same thing." I smiled.

"You're not supposed to answer a question with a question, but that's fair. I'm out here because it's a pretty afternoon and I was tired of being all cooped up in my house. So I put a few pieces of leftover chicken and a biscuit in a lunch sack and decided to go for a ride. Now, your turn."

"I left my home in Stone Coal this morning, heading to Ashland, and I got hungry so I stopped here to eat a bite and stretch my legs."

"There's got to be more to it than that," said Miss Charlene. "Why are you going to Ashland, and where in the world is Stone Coal?"

"Well, Stone Coal is where I'm from and Ashland is where I'm headed. I hope to look somebody up."

"Oh, you are a man of mystery. Do you mind if I smoke?" She pulled one of those long skinny cigarettes from her purse, lit it, and blew perfectly shaped smoke rings in my direction.

"Nice smoke rings," I observed.

"I am very, very talented," Charlene said slowly and deliberately, "especially with my lips."

"I can see."

"Oh, you have no idea."

"Oh . . ." I said.

"Lewis Ray Jacobs," she started finger-walking up my thigh beginning just above my kneecap, "I could teach a young boy like you a lesson that would last him a lifetime." She stopped strategically just short of . . . well, just short.

"I'm going to guess that a lesson such as that would not come free, would it Miss Devine?"

"It's Charlene. And honey, nothing worth having comes without a price. That's the free part of the lesson right there." She giggled.

"You couldn't have caught me at a worse time, Charlene. I don't know if I have enough money to get to Ashland and back home even. So I guess I'll have to pass on any educational opportunities for now."

"You know," Charlene said, smiling, "you're so young and handsome, I'm tempted to bend the rules just this once. You sure would thank Miss Charlene, and some little girl someday would too."

"How tempted are you?" I asked, trying to maintain the flirt.

"Not tempted enough, I'm afraid."

Charlene scooted off the edge of the picnic table and dusted the seat of her dress as she walked toward her car.

"One other thing," I yelled after her. "How do I get to Ashland?"

"You're heading in the right direction." She waved and blew a kiss as she drove away.

Travis would love this one, I thought—my almost encounter with a hooker. It hit me with a rawness anew of just how much I missed my friend.

Following Miss Devine's instruction, I continued north on good old US 23 and hoped that eventually I would find Ashland. In the late afternoon I spied a Gulf station and pulled the Comet up to the pumps.

"Fill er up?" An old man ambled out, spitting tobacco juice in the gravel at his feet.

"Yes, with regular," I said, counting my money for at least the third time since this morning. Having not spent anything as of yet, predictably the count remained constant.

"Check under the hood?" He spit again.

"If you don't mind." I started to count again, then stopped myself.

In a few minutes I settled my bill and continued north on US 23.

CHAPTER TEN

July 24, 1987

"What's your name?" A waif of a child rounded the house from the direction of the restaurant, taking long strides on rail-thin legs. Gracie had gone back inside to refresh our teas and find us some "leavins," her term for leftovers. Though I wasn't at all hungry, Gracie insisted that we eat a bite. The boy, who couldn't have been much more than ten, was skinny as a tobacco stick and pale as a celery heart. He had long strands of thin blonde hair tucked behind his protruding ears.

"My name's Lewis Ray. What's yours?"

"Jesse Lee. Where's Gracie?"

"She went inside to get us a bite to eat."

"It's a little late for lunch," Jesse Lee observed.

"Well, I got here late and I guess I held Gracie up," I admitted.

"What are you doing here?" Jesse sat on the concrete slab of the back porch, much as Opp had the first time we had talked about my buying his car.

"I'm here for a funeral."

"Who died?"

"Just someone I used to know."

"Well, you must still know them or you wouldn't be coming to their funeral. My poppy died when I was eight. I went to his funeral. Didn't look much like him."

"Was your poppy your grandfather?"

"The kids at school say I'm a bastert."

"A what?"

"A bastert. You see, I don't got a daddy, so I'm a bastert."

"Oh, a bastard?"

"Yep, a bastert. Gracie says them kids that call me a bastert are shitheads, except she spells it out."

"I bet she does. Gracie is a good friend to have."

"You ain't just shittin' mister. Of course I can't say shittin' in front of Gracie. She threatens to wash my mouth out with lye soap. Gracie is the best. I come down here every single afternoon and check on her. She says an old woman like her could up and die and not a soul would know til the buzzards started circling. During the school year I stop by every day when the bus lets me off, and when I'm out of school for the summer I come by too. We just live up the holler a ways."

"Did you live with your poppy?"

"Yep, me and Mommy and Poppy, til he died."

"And your poppy was your grandfather?"

"Some kids at school say I'm worse than a bastert cause my poppy was my daddy. He's really my mommy's daddy, not mine, but the kids at school say he was my daddy too. Mommy has a name for those kids and she don't spell it out neither."

"I'll just bet she doesn't."

About that time the screen door bumped open and Gracie backed out of the kitchen and onto the stoop, carrying a tray of lunch meat sandwiches, chips, and cookies.

"Well, I see you met Jesse Lee," Gracie said as she sat the tray down on a small round metal table. "He's the one looks after me now that Opp's gone. I always tell him, an old woman like me could up and die and nobody'd ever know til the buzzards started circling. So Jesse comes every day to make sure I don't wake up dead some morning." Gracie's smile made her eyes disappear. "Jesse Lee, I put a couple of plates of food on the sideboard for you and your mommy, so don't go off and leave them or you'll be without supper."

"Yes ma'am," Jesse Lee said obediently.

"Now where was we?" Gracie continued.

"Oh, I was yammering on about this and that," I said, not quite sure if Gracie wanted to know more or was just being nice.

"Where you from, mister?" Jesse Lee butted in.

"I live in Nashville now."

"Do you know Hank Junior, Old Bocephus?" Jesse Lee asked. "My mommy loves him. We play his tapes all the time."

"No, the country music stars and I don't travel much in the same circles."

"I'm going to be on the Opry someday," Jesse Lee said without reservation.

"Oh, do you play an instrument?"

"Nope. I'm gonna be a singing star, just like Hank Junior."

"So you can sing?"

"Don't know. Never tried. But it don't look all that hard."

"Now you go on Jesse Lee, and take your mommy's supper to her," Gracie interrupted. "Me and Mr. Jacobs here have things to catch up on."

"Yessum," Jesse Lee responded with obvious courtesy and respect. He went into the house and returned with two Melmac plates heaped high and covered with aluminum foil.

"Good to meet you mister," Jesse Lee said as he headed across the yard. "I'll be back to check on you tomorrow, Gracie," he shouted over his shoulder as he disappeared down the path leading through the garden.

"I see you're still taking in strays." I smiled at Gracie.

"Ah lordy, he's just a poor child up against it. He and his mommy live up the holler a ways. Most days I try to put them back a few leavins so at least they'll have something for supper."

"Like I said . . . still taking in strays."

"Jesse Lee ain't exactly a stray. You make it sound like he's a three-legged kitten somebody set off beside the road on me."

"Gracie, we were all strays. Kids who wandered in, whether by luck or by design. And you took care of us. I didn't realize it at the time, but all of us who hung out here were pretty much a bunch of misfits. Just look at us—me, Travis, Johnny Frank, Linda, just to name a few."

"Young man, you were not misfits and I won't have you talking about yourself or any of them other younguns like that." Gracie became stern. "You all were my kids and I needed you as much as you needed me, just like little Jesse Lee. No, he ain't going to be the prom king, but he has a heart big as a canebrake and his turn is sweet as a plum granny. And it does give me some assurance to know that at least once a day somebody is going to come by to make sure I ain't laid out in the floor with a broke hip, or worse."

"Gracie, I'll say it til the day I die, they broke the mold when they made you."

"Oh, hush that foolishness." Gracie leaned closer. "There is one thing I think we need to talk about before you show up at that funeral home though."

"What's that?"

"They was a lot of talk after you left here. Most of it died down over the years, but, it's starting to come up again."

"Talk about what?"

"Just nosey, gossipy stuff that's none of nobody's business. But you need to know. One thing leads to another and then people make stuff up in their minds." Gracie uncharacteristically avoided eye contact.

"What kind of stuff?"

"Well, I guess the best way through a ten-acre baccer patch is right through the middle, ain't it?"

✳ ✳ ✳

September 6, 1967

Just as the sun was setting low in the evening sky, it occurred to me that I had made no plans for where I would spend the night. A motel was out of the question, but luckily the weather was mild, so a blanket, a pillow, and the back seat seemed the logical choice. The only decision to be made was just where to pull off for my overnight. According to the signs I was less than sixty miles from Ashland, and since I really didn't know where I was going once I got there, I thought it best to be on the lookout for a roadside park. Surely I could find one somewhere between here and there. The next sign indicated I had entered Sciota County, Kentucky, which sounded like an Indian name to me. And then I came to the town of Sciota Furnace.

"Sciiiiooooota Furnace," I said aloud, drawing out each syllable.

As I was amusing myself and pondering the origin of the oddly named town, I noticed a glow of brightly colored lights up ahead on the horizon. I continued on and before long the valley opened up to reveal an expanse of farmland, soon to be fallow for the coming winter. In the middle of this bottom I discovered the source of the bright lights to be a sprawling carnival, which covered at least five acres, as measured by my only frame of reference, a tobacco patch of roughly the same size just east of Stone Coal. Unlike this region, five-acre fields were few and far between in Pratt County.

A more perfect coincidence could not have befallen me, I fig-ured: an evening's entertainment, a place for a cheap supper, and a crowded field in which to park, amongst the trucks and trailers waiting at the ready to transport the carnival to the next small burg. My car, with a sleeping teenager in the back seat, would hardly be noticed. I slowly drove past the empty vehicles of the locals, who would be taking their leave once the neon lights were turned off and the whining generators were shut down. I followed the flattened grass tracks to the back of the field and parked the Comet between two large aluminum semitrailers, the sides of which were emblazoned with red lettering proclaiming "Farber Brothers Shows." I couldn't imagine a more suitable place to settle in for the night.

After I got out of my car I unbuckled my pants and re-tucked my shirt in the privacy afforded me by the empty trailers, and once again counted my money. Having been warned of unsavory sorts associated with traveling carnivals, I relocated my wallet to my front pants pocket where I could keep a hand on it at all times. The sun had just set as I headed down the midway, and the multicolored lights of the flashing neon tubes transformed this rural pasture into a fantasyland.

"Hey good-lookin'," a girl called from the Guessing Booth.

I waved and kept on walking.

"I said, hey good-lookin'," she repeated.

This time I stopped and looked at her more closely.

"Hey yourself," I said as I approached her tent.

"Twenty-five cents and I'll make a guess. If I'm wrong you'll win a prize." She smiled.

The guessing girl couldn't be much older than I, and she was extremely pretty—tall and willowy, with dark hair cropped short and worn close. She had skin like milk glass and her round eyes were a deep chestnut brown. She wore tight jeans, cowboy boots, and what could have been a man's red cotton shirt pulled tight and knotted just above her waist, yielding an occasional glimpse of her navel.

"Guess what?" I inquired.

"Oh, just about anything. Age and weight are my best, but with a little luck I can probably get the month you were born or your zodiac sign. Stuff like that. I can also read your cards, but that costs extra."

"Why would I want you to guess stuff I already know? Besides, I could always lie."

"What's your name, cowboy?"

"Lewis Ray. What's yours?"

"Kissimmee." She smiled.

"Kissimmee, like the city in Florida?"

"No, just Kissimmee like Kissimmee," she said, still smiling.

"Is that where you're from?" I asked.

"Could be. Where are you from?"

"You ought to be able to guess that." I laughed.

"Don't kid a kidder, cowboy. You hand over a quarter and we'll see what I can come up with."

"I'll give you one for free. I'm from Stone Coal, down in the mountains."

"Well Stone Coal, what brings you way up here to river country?"

"Hard to say," I admitted in all truth.

"Hey sweet lady, let me guess your age." Kissimmee smiled at a passing local who just looked away and kept on walking, two children in tow.

"Slow tonight," I observed.

"It's early. The rubes haven't had time to wash off the factory grease and foundry grime yet. They'll be here."

"Well Kissimmee, I'm going to get me a cotton candy and a corn dog and take in the Farber Brothers Shows. Hope you do a lot of good guessing tonight."

"You take care, Stone Coal. A boy from East Kentucky could get lost in a place big as this." She laughed. "Hey good-lookin', let me guess your weight," she yelled at a passing gawker.

The midway was filled with freak shows and peep shows, and as the night wore on Kissimmee's prediction turned out to be true. The yokels came out in force. Men with their wives lined up to see the two-headed calf and men without their wives lined up to see Lola la Farge, direct from Paris, France.

"Come on gentlemen," the barker yelled. "Lola wants to see all of you, and you can see *all of Lola*," he continued with a wink.

"How about you, young man?" The barker picked me out of the crowded field of mostly middle-aged men. "Stand back, you old fellows, and let this young man to the front of the line. One thing we can all do for the younger generation is to make sure they know sexy when they see it. Come on up here, young man. For a mere one-dollar bill you can see the very lady that has played the Moolah Rouge in Paris, France, the lovely Lola la Farge."

I shook my head no and wormed my way to the back of the horde of freshly bathed and shaved blue-collars.

At the end of the midway was an arched entry announcing, in what must have been five hundred colored lightbulbs, "Funland." Inside, young children were waiting, tickets in hand, queued for the next turnover of carousel riders. Others were handing over their dimes at the Duck Pond, in hopes of picking the elusive waterfowl marked "choice" on the bottom, thus entitling them to claim the giant stuffed panda suspended from the tent's apex. However, Chinese finger traps seemed to be all that was actually being won.

Teenage boys, girlfriends on their arms, were lined up at the basketball hoops and the rifle range, with aspirations of winning teddy bears for their dates. This could be any small town in the mountain coalfields, I thought, as I breathed in the mixed aroma of scorched popcorn, funnel cake, and cotton candy.

"I'll take a corn dog and a Grapeade." I leaned up to the screened window of the restaurant on wheels. Waddled arms took my money and delivered my order as the screen slid open and closed.

The Rock-O-Plane had the longest line and I watched the carney work the crowd as I finished my corn dog and chomped on the last of my grape-flavored ice. I heard the screams of the teenage girls and the coarse yells of the pubescent boys as the cages went round and round on their axles, all the while orbiting the ride's flashing hub and streaming neon ribbons through the night sky. I remembered how Travis and I would ride the Rock-O-Plane until we nearly threw up, then stagger through the fairground like two drunkards.

Reaching the end of Funland, I wound my way back to the midway past the tent of Lola la Farge and that of Fatty Faye Falaffle, who purportedly weighed in at over five hundred and thirty-five pounds. At the Guessing Booth I saw a large group of people gathered around Kissimmee, mostly gawking men who had probably just left the tent of Lola and were admiring a much younger, much prettier, albeit much more clothed attraction than Miss la Farge.

"This is just not my night!" Kissimmee exclaimed. "Who's next? Hey there, handsome." She nodded at a rube who shyly looked around to make sure it was indeed he that she was addressing. "Step right up here."

Obeying as if he were a schoolboy, the thirtyish-aged man handed Kissimmee a quarter and stood on the wooden box in the center of the tent.

"Now what am I guessing?" Kissimmee took his baseball cap and put it on her own head.

"I don't know, I guess my weight."

In my observation this guy could not have weighed over a hundred and fifty pounds.

"Well let's see," Kissimmee continued. "Make a muscle for me, handsome." He flexed his lean arm, much as Popeye would, and Kissimmee kneaded his puny bicep.

"Oh my, a muscular one you are," she said, returning his cap.

"Now let me feel your ribs." She planted her palms firmly on his waist, just above his hips, and pushed and pulled a couple of times.

"Slow down, tiger," she exclaimed, as if it were he rather than she who initiated the hip thrusts. The crowd roared as the skinny bumpkin turned a deep shade of red.

"I'm guessing you'd weigh in at one hundred eight-five. Am I right?"

"Not close," he said, grinning broadly. "I weigh a hundred and sixty pounds first thing in the morning stark naked."

"Well I'd like to see that." Kissimmee raised her eyebrows. "Don't make me get out the scales and strip you down right here in front of all these nice folks." Kissimmee handed him a Kewpie doll as she admitted defeat.

"Okay handsome, I can't let you quit while I'm down, give me another quarter and we'll double or nothing for a teddy bear."

"Alright." He fished through his pockets and eventually counted out two dimes and a nickel from a handful of change.

"How about your age within two years?"

"Alright," he said again, grinning like a summer possum.

"Let me look a little closer." Kissimmee slowly walked around the rigid bean pole, eyeing him from top to bottom.

"You're going to have to help me a little. Are you married?"

"Nope."

"You mean a muscular young hunk like you hasn't been caught yet? You hear that, ladies? This one's a keeper. How about it, girls? Anybody want to turn this Guessing Booth into an auction? Highest bidder gets to take Tex here, home."

Again, the crowd cheered and the red-faced man looked at his feet as he shuffled from one foot to the other.

"Now handsome, you do have a driver's license on you, don't you?"

"Yep." He nodded.

"Okay. You pick anybody in the crowd and give them your license to hold for a minute." Kissimmee waved her outstretched arm over the gathering indicating the myriad of choices available to him, and he chose a heavyset woman in a Silver Dollar City sweatshirt near the front of the crowd.

"Now, I'm going to write a number on this piece of paper," Kissimmee announced, as she pulled a pad and marker from the chair behind her. She positioned herself so that no one in the audience could see the pad, and with the marker appeared to write a number. She then handed the pad, facedown, to the sweatshirted lady who was the keeper of the driver's license.

"You look like an honest person," Kissimmee continued. "Just how old is this fine-looking specimen here on the pedestal?"

"Uh, I don't know. It says here he was borned in 1940. How old would that make him?" Again, the crowd laughed.

"If my math doesn't fail me, I'd say he is twenty-seven years old. Is that right, good-lookin'?" Kissimmee addressed the skinny man who was the center of attention.

"Yep, this past July," he declared, beaming.

"Okay, now madam, would you be so kind as to show the audience the number that I wrote on the pad I just handed you?"

The amazed woman held the pad high, displaying a neatly inscribed *two* and *seven*. She turned as if on a carousel, for all to see. Everyone in the crowd applauded, but none more exuberantly than the skinny man in the center of the tent who had just lost fifty cents.

"Alright, who's next?" Kissimmee surveyed the crowd. "For one thin quarter I can guess your weight, age, birth month, or you throw something at me and we'll see if I can guess it. Come on, I need a sucker, er, I mean customer."

"How about me?" I shouted from the back of the crowd.

"Well come right up here and let's get a little closer, if you know what I mean."

The crowd parted as I made my way up to the wooden box in the center of the tent.

"Oh my goodness, you are a good-looking thing," Kissimmee gushed. "I'm not going to even guess your age, cause that would make what most of us girls are thinking illegal, am I right, girls?"

The females in the crowd shouted their approval.

"Okay, then what are you gonna guess?" I asked.

"You choose, big boy." Kissimmee looked me over as if for the first time. "Now, tell these good people gathered here, have you and I ever met before?"

"No ma'am," I lied.

"Well, if we had I know I would have remembered it." Kissimmee assumed a sultry voice. "And I'm sure you would have too." She winked to the crowd.

"Okay," I said, "why don't you guess my hometown—where I'm from."

"Oh that one will cost you fifty cents." Kissimmee smiled.

"Fifty cents it is," I said, flipping her a shiny Kennedy half-dollar.

"We'll need a volunteer from the audience. I'm looking for a sweet young girl who might be able to tend to this handsome boy's needs once I take his money. Any takers?"

A pretty blonde girl, probably close to my own age, and clearly a crowd favorite, came forward and took a curtsy. The audience cheered her with a familiarity that made me think she must be one of the popular kids at the local high school.

"What's your name, sweetie?" Kissimmee asked.

"Rachel," the cute blonde responded.

"Rachel, have you ever met this good-looking piece of manhood here, before?"

"Nope." She giggled nervously.

"Would you like to get to know him better now?"

"I don't know. I guess." More giggles.

"Handsome, what is your name?" Kissimmee asked.

"Lewis Ray Jacobs," I said.

"Okay, Lewis Ray, hand Rachel here your driver's license."

I obeyed.

"Rachel, is he telling the truth so far? Is he Lewis Ray?"

"That's what it says on his license," Rachel said.

"Now let's see," Kissimmee continued, "I'm thinking by his boyish charm and southern drawl that Lewis Ray here isn't a local. Especially since Rachel doesn't know him, and I believe Rachel would make it her business to know him if he were from around here. Am I right about that, Rachel?" Again the crowd cheered and Rachel nodded her head in agreement.

"Rachel, is Lewis Ray from Kentucky?"

"Yes he is," Rachel confirmed.

"Well, since this is Kentucky, I imagine you all are thinking that was just a lucky guess, and rightly so," Kissimmee continued. "But that wasn't the deal was it, tall, dark and handsome?" She nodded at me. "I need to come up with your hometown."

"That's right." I continued the ruse.

"Well, I'm thinking it is two names. Am I right, Rachel?"

"Absolutely," Rachel said with perhaps a hint of skepticism.

"Two names. Let me see." Kissimmee put her forefingers to her temples and began slow circular motions as if to channel some sort of psychic energy. "Yes, two names. One is Coal and the other is Rock . . . or Slate . . . no, wait. The other is Stone. It's coming to me now, Coal Stone . . . er, no . . ."

"Stone Coal!" Rachel shouted. "He's from Stone Coal."

The crowd cheered loudly as Kissimmee took a bow. She then dramatically swept her arm toward Rachel and me, and following her lead, we bowed to the appreciative crowd as well.

"Now Rachel, you and Lewis Ray here go and ride the Octopus on me." Kissimmee handed me a token good for a ride on any attraction at the carnival.

Rachel and I walked to the back of the crowd as Kissimmee continued her banter with the audience.

"Was that a setup?" Rachel asked as we cleared the crowded midway aisle.

"Absolutely not," I said, feigning indignation.

"Well, whatever, it was fun. And you owe me a ride on the Octopus."

"Okay," I said as we headed back to Funland. "You know everything about me, so tell me about Rachel."

"Not much to know. I live in Sciota Furnace, go to Sciota County High, I'm seventeen years old, and my boyfriend is an absolute asshole."

"Aha! The asshole boyfriend. That's why you're at the carnival unescorted."

"Oh yes. He was at the carnival last night, but he wasn't unescorted. Asshole."

"I'm beginning to see. If the pretty girl Rachel is seen at the carnival with a mysterious stranger and word gets back to the asshole boyfriend then the pretty girl Rachel gets her revenge."

"You're not only handsome, but you're smart too." Rachel hooked her arm in mine as we strolled under the Funland sign. A few rides later Rachel gave me a peck on the cheek, thanked me for a fun evening, and headed toward the parking lot.

The night was winding down as I headed back to my car to settle in for a little shut-eye. Most of the families had deserted the midway. A few men were still hanging around the entrance to Lola la Farge's tent, awaiting what was billed as the Grand Finale Experience of the Day. As I passed the Guessing Booth the lights were off and Kissimmee was lacing down the sides of the tent.

"Hey, Stone Coal. Never took you for a ringer." Kissimmee was pulling the ties tight and expertly forming clove hitches to secure the flaps. "Guess you want your money back, huh?"

"Oh no. It was worth half a dollar to see the looks on the faces of the spectators."

"It's all in the show, Stone Coal."

"Lewis, Lewis Ray." I corrected her.

"That is more boring than my real name, so now you're Stone Coal."

"Okay, but just to be fair, what is your real name?"

"You want to go get a cup of coffee?" Kissimmee gave the last knot a final tug.

"Sure, I'll have some coffee."

I followed Kissimmee to a ragged tent behind the trailer that housed the Farber Brothers offices. A few rows of tables were set up and surrounded by wooden folding chairs, much like the ones the funeral home brings in for overflow seating at wakes and services back in Stone Coal. The tent was empty except for a beer-bellied guy in a greasy white tee shirt who was sitting behind a makeshift counter of plywood laid strategically across stacked Pepsi cases. He peered up from his paperback.

"Hey, Cookie. Two coffees please."

"Seriously? Cookie?" I looked at Kissimmee.

"Every cook in every carnival in every rathole town in America is named Cookie." Kissimmee smiled. "It comes with the job."

A study in slow motion, Cookie got up and crossed the cramped kitchen area and drew two cups of coffee from a giant chrome urn.

"There you go, sweetie," he said as he plopped down the two steaming mugs. "That's twenty cents."

Kissimmee flipped a quarter to Cookie and nodded for me to follow her to the corner table.

"Is this where you take your meals?" I asked, surveying the tent.

"Only if I have to. This is the carnival's kitchen for the workers, but I usually pick up a burger on the midway or heat up a can of soup in my trailer."

"I've never met a . . ."

"Carney? That's alright. Carney is fine. It's not a bad word."

"Okay, I've never met a carney before."

"Well, we're not Gypsies and we don't pick your pockets and we don't steal your babies. We are just working people who travel with the carnival to make a living."

"How old are you?"

"Twenty. You?"

"Almost eighteen."

"You look older."

"You look younger."

"Yep, I get that a lot."

"So you're twenty years old and travel with the carnival by yourself. No family? Just you?"

"Most of the time just me." She continued, "My entire family is in the business, though. My brother runs a shy. That's carnival for he has a game. Mom and Dad are semiretired and my sister and her husband have a couple of zamps."

"Zamps?" I asked.

"Kiddie rides. We have our own language. We are all small businesses and we pay the show that we travel with, either a percentage or a flat fee for rent. Different shows have different arrangements."

"How did you learn to guess stuff?"

"That's the easiest con going. You don't. People give you a quarter to make a guess. If you get lucky you keep their money. If you miss you give them a Kewpie doll that you paid a nickel for. Do the math." Kissimmee laughed.

"Okay, how did you guess that hayseed's age?"

"Mostly luck. And after a while you get fairly good at it, but it's all about the show. Making people laugh and have a good time. They can forget about their troubles for at least a little while. If you haven't noticed, the carnival crowd isn't exactly the jet set."

"You aren't what I expected," I admitted.

"How so?"

"Well for starters, you're gorgeous."

"Don't stop."

"And you're smart," I continued.

"Okay, stop before you say I'm also clean."

"I have a long history of putting my foot in my mouth, so thanks for stopping me while I'm ahead." I laughed.

"Carneys run the gamut," Kissimmee continued, "but many of us are just like you, only we travel around making our living. My folks live in Florida."

"Let me guess. In Kissimmee."

"Okay, my parents live in Kissimmee. We are all together from around Thanksgiving til about Easter and then we head out with the shows for the season. So, now you know. Tell me again how gorgeous I am. I liked that part."

"Oh, gee." I felt my cheeks redden. "I'm not usually very good with words. It just came out."

"Well, it was nice. Thank you." Kissimmee patted my knee.

"Tell me about you," she continued.

"There's really not much to tell. I live down in the mountains with my mother and sister. My best friend, who has been like my brother, had a real run of bad luck and he and I are on the outs. I think he is sleeping with my girlfriend. Some other guy I ran into this summer, it turns out just may be my brother, and I would like to find my dad, whom I haven't seen in nearly ten years."

"And you thought I had a story to tell?"

"I'll admit it sounds pretty wild when I actually say it out loud."

"Stone Coal,"—Kissimmee looked at me with the prettiest eyes I could ever, ever remember seeing—"would you like to sleep with me tonight?"

"Good lord I would indeed."

"When I say sleep, I mean just that. Sleep."

"Okay," I said, "my other option is the back seat of my car, so I'm thinking whatever you have in mind is a step up."

I followed Kissimmee as she wound through the maze of trailers and truck campers until we came to her home on the road, a small silver Airstream hooked to a pickup truck, the bed of which was covered with a green tarp.

"This is it," she said as she unlocked the door.

"You can get everything in this?" I motioned to the truck.

"Sure. The tent rolls up and packs into a duffel and the poles and ropes fit in right next to it. Then the lights and the sign go in, and on top of that the boxes of prizes. I cover it all with the tarp, tie it down, and I'm off and running."

Kissimmee opened the door of the trailer and went in first.

"Wait, I'll get the light." She disappeared into the darkness. In a moment a dim bulb revealed a tiny cabin with a bed across the back, a two-burner stove atop an open cabinet, a single-basin sink, a narrow door concealing what I guessed was a bathroom, and nothing more.

"Okay Stone Coal, have you ever smoked reefer?" Kissimmee asked, as she pulled a small silk pouch from under the bed.

"No, I smoked cigarettes once and got sick as a dog."

"Well this ain't going to make you sick. And don't think just cause I've got a little weed I'm some good-for-nothing raghead."

"What's a raghead?" I asked innocently.

"Sorry. Carney talk for Gypsy."

"So carneys don't like Gypsies?"

"Not so much we don't like them, we just don't want to be confused with them. The carnival world has its own unique pecking order."

Kissimmee deftly held a single leaf of OCB rolling paper in her left hand, retrieved a pinch of dried herb from the pouch and crumbled it into the thin white membrane, and then with a few skillful maneuvers, produced a perfectly rolled joint.

"You've done this before," I observed.

"A girl has to be good at something besides guessing crap." Kissimmee laughed.

"Now," she continued, "watch me. I'm going to light up this doobie and take a long hard pull and hold it in my lungs as long as I can. I'm going to slowly exhale and I'm going to hand it to you and you do the same thing. Got it?"

"I guess."

After a few false starts and a couple of coughing fits I finally got the hang of it, and within minutes I was in the warm glow of my first cannabis high. Kissimmee stripped down to her panties and bra, revealing exactly what I had imagined—a slender, perfect body.

"Okay Stone Coal," she said as she slid beneath the worn covers of her narrow bed, "you can strip down to your skivvies if you'd like, but you are going to keep your drawers on and everything that's contained within those drawers is going to stay right where it is. Understand?"

"Uh, yep," I said. Within seconds I was sitting on the edge of the bed, naked except for my BVDs.

"Here you go." She patted the bed beside her and I slid in as instructed. Kissimmee pulled my arm around her bare shoulder and nestled into my chest. So just like that, there we were, cuddled, and soon her breathing became steady and even.

"Stone Coal."

"Yes?"

"Don't even think about groping my tits."

"Okay."

"Goodnight."

"Goodnight."

✳ ✳ ✳

I awoke to unfamiliar surroundings and was immediately aware of the stuffiness of a small space. Closer inspection and clearer thinking brought back memories of Kissimmee and the night before. My last recollections were of the mellowing effects of the weed and the rhythm of our synchronized breathing as I drifted off to sleep. I swung my feet over the side of the bed and sat upright for a moment, getting my bearings, then realized I was alone. Hoping to find a toilet, I slid back the narrow bi-fold door. There was a small commode and an even smaller washbasin. I relieved myself and splashed some cold water on my face then located my clothes piled near the foot of the single bed. Just as I finished dressing the door to the trailer opened, and a fresh cool breeze drifted in, along with Kissimmee.

"Hey Stone Coal, I thought you were going to sleep all day." She smelled of lilac, and her hair was still wet.

"You didn't take a shower in that bathroom, did you?" I said, nodding toward the toilet.

"That's not a bathroom, it's called a head."

"Well if it's not a bathroom, I just peed in your head."

"That's what it's for, and nothing more." Kissimmee laughed. "The carnival has a bathhouse. Feel free if you want. The men's is just at the end of the row of trailers behind the cook tent. Better hurry, the hot water gets gone fast."

"I'll be okay," I said. "I'll freshen up later somewhere along the road."

"You never did say where you were headed."

"Probably cause I'm not quite sure. But I'm thinking I need to get to Ashland."

"If you need directions, always ask a carney. We know every back road and shortcut in every podunk town in the south. Get back out on twenty-three and stay north. You'll cross the river into West Virginia at Kenova. Keep on following the river road and you'll cross back over into Kentucky at Ashland. You're less than an hour away."

"Thanks," I said. "That should get me there. And thanks for letting me sleep with you. Beats the hell out of being alone in the back seat."

"Well it sure was nice to wake up in your arms this morning. Stone Coal, you are a sweet, sweet guy. I hate to see you go. If you ever see the Farber Brothers Shows in some jake town cornfield, look me up. I'll guess your name."

Kissimmee walked with me to the parking lot and strolled alongside my car as I slowly rolled down the drive toward the highway.

"Hey Stone Coal, do you still want to know my real name?" she called as the distance between us widened.

"I already do," I shouted back. "It's Kissimmee, and it's fabulous."

CHAPTER ELEVEN

For the next hour I followed the meandering road toward Ashland. My mind kept replaying the previous night at the carnival, and mostly the parts with Kissimmee. Reality soon took hold though, and I began to feel like I was in far over my head on this journey. Ashland turned out to be a much larger city than I had anticipated. As I crossed the river I saw tall smokestacks belching plumes of blue-white clouds skyward and the air took on the smell of burning rubber. How to even begin to find my father in this huge industrial maze of a city was overwhelming, and I came to the sad realization of just how ill-conceived my idea had been.

I pulled my car into the parking lot of a large foundry. Vehicles were filed row after row after row practically as far as the eye could see. Just in front of a guard shack at the entrance to the plant, and under a sign that announced admittance for "Employees Only," sat a diner truck made of highly polished stainless steel. The long side door was propped open, providing a canopy under which stood a short stout man wearing a white apron and a soda jerk cap. He was leaned up against the counter and was reading from a newspaper. Not able to find a parking spot, I stopped in front of his enterprise and got out.

"You can't park there, son," said the proprietor. "In about ten minutes this area will be filled with people on break, and I'll be busier than a pair of jumper cables at a hillbilly funeral."

"I'll just be a minute," I replied. "I just need some advice."

"Well I ain't Dear Abby, but I'll give it a shot."

"If I were to be looking for someone and have little information about them, what would you suggest?"

"I hate to be too obvious, but did you try the phone book?"

"Yep. No luck. Ashland's a big place."

"You got that right. A big old industrial city with people coming and going like bees from a honey tree," the white-hatted man continued. "Not that it's my business, but who is it you're looking for?"

"My dad. I haven't seen him since 1958 and all I know is he's a welder by trade and was last known to be living around Ashland."

"Wow, you don't have much, do you? Ashland is a big place, but around Ashland is a much bigger place," he said, emphasizing the word much. "You might try the union hall."

"Union hall?"

"United Ironworkers. It's a big federation. Welders, ironworkers, pipefitters . . . they all belong to it if they work any union jobs in this area. It's strong here. It may or may not get you anywhere, but it's a start."

"Thanks a lot," I said. "Where is this union hall?"

"Pretty close by. I have a stop there every afternoon at three forty-five, just as the day-shift guys are coming by to check tomorrow's work board. Get back out on Blaine Street, go down one, two, three—six lights and turn right on Willow. Willow T-bones into Clifton. Turn right on Clifton and you will see the union hall on your left. Can't miss it."

"Thanks," I said. "It's a good start."

I pulled back onto Blaine, counted the lights, made the turns, and amazingly ended up at the United Ironworkers of America Local 452, a rather nondescript storefront stuck in amongst a row of small garages and tool and die shops that lined both sides of the street. I entered the arched doorway where a sign hung that proclaimed "Eight Hours Work for Eight Hours Pay." The union hall was a big room, bisected by a counter running its entire width. Behind the counter was a scattering of cluttered desks, all empty save for one. A good-sized woman with red hair and redder lipstick and thick glasses perched toward the end of her pudgy nose was pecking on an old manual typewriter. She glanced sideways at me, but continued her typing. In a bit she pushed her glasses up, stood from her desk, and waddled to the counter.

"What can I help you with, honey?"

"Well, I'm trying to find somebody and I don't have a whole lot of information on him. I think he's a welder and he works in this area. Someone suggested I check with you," I said in the most courteous and persuasive tone I could muster.

"Me personally? Someone told you that I, Cora Reed, could help you?" she asked with a trace of attitude. This wasn't starting off well, I thought.

"No, not you personally, but they said the union might be a good place to start."

"If whoever you're looking for is a member of the local here, I will have a card on him, but we are very careful about handing out information on our members. We get ex-wives, ex-girlfriends, ex-boyfriends, the law, bail bondsmen, bounty hunters—honey you name it and they've come through that door hoping I can give 'em what they need. More often than not I send 'em away empty-handed."

"What would I need to do to get you to help me, Miss Reed?" I was trying to appear as young and naive as possible. The naive part was certainly not a problem.

"Well a court order or subpoena would definitely get you anything I got, but I'm betting that ain't the case is it?" Cora pushed her glasses back up on her nose.

"No ma'am."

"Okay, gimme your best shot and I'll decide if it's good enough."

I decided to play it straight. I had nothing to lose and I couldn't make anything up that would be any more convincing than the truth.

"I'm looking for my father. I'm not sure I'd recognize him if he walked through that door. He left when I was eight years old. I have driven from Stone Coal, a little town about one hundred fifty miles from here. I have no idea what I will say to him, and I really don't know why I'm trying to find him, but it just seemed like the right time to try."

"Go on." Cora nodded.

"Go on? That's it. There is no more to the story," I said.

"There's got to be more. A kid your age don't just up and drive a hundred and fifty miles with little or nothing to go on if there ain't more. But . . . I guess that's none of my beeswax now is it? Are you still in school?"

"Yep, just started my senior year."

"What is your daddy's name, honey?" Cora asked, without giving any indication as to whether she was going to help me.

"CB Jacobs. Charles Billy, but he goes by CB, so it may be under CB or Charles or Billy, I really don't know."

Cora slowly waddled to a bank of file drawers that looked much like the card catalogue at the Bosco High library, only about twice as large. After pulling out a long narrow drawer, she deftly fingered through the cards and eventually settled on one near the middle of the tray. Cora approached the counter, card in hand.

"Honey, I'm not allowed to give out any information," she said apologetically. She then placed the card facedown on the counter along with a pencil and a piece of scrap paper.

"I'm going to the restroom now, and you'd best be gone when I get back. Understand?"

I nodded.

✳ ✳ ✳

Okay, now what, I thought as I drove aimlessly through the streets of Ashland. I had everything I needed except a reason to pursue this undertaking. I really had no idea what I hoped to accomplish, but on the other hand, I had nothing to lose and no cause to turn back now.

Russell, Kentucky, was a little burg not far from Ashland; the man at the filling station had said just follow the river and don't blink. According to the union card, Charles Billy Jacobs lived at 611 White Oak Creek Road. It was nearly three o'clock in the afternoon when I passed a sign confirming that I had indeed reached Russell. Yellow buses lumbered through the streets and traffic was at all but a standstill as young children, book bags and lunch pails in hand, made their way home from a day at school.

White Oak Creek Road was not difficult to find, since all streets branched out from the town square. Soon I was scanning mailboxes looking for number 611. The houses were all similar in appearance: small, shotgun, and most were up on stilts, suggesting that White Oak Creek often overflowed its banks. As was typical of the other homes situated along the creek's edge, 611 was a framed structure perched atop cinder block pylons, with room enough underneath to park a car. However, no car was present.

I pulled into the sparsely graveled drive, got out, ascended the steep front steps, and pecked on the window. I held my breath and waited. I had prepared myself for no one being home, but none-theless, I was anxious. Suddenly, I heard movement from within. I somehow managed not to turn and run, but I sure as hell didn't have the courage to knock again. I stood there hoping that I was mistaken—maybe I had just imagined the noise—but no, there was definitely somebody stirring in there. I heard the click of a latch as someone on the other side was unlocking the door. My heart was now racing and my face felt like it was on fire. I could not believe that

I was about to be face-to-face with my father—a man I hardly knew, but one with whom I shared blood and bone. I felt the breath leave my body entirely as the door opened, and there stood Paul Jenkins.

At first I was paralyzed. I could not move nor speak. I heard a loud groan and realized it was coming from me.

"Well I'll be shit" was all I could think to say.

"Hey man," Paul said, looking at his feet. "This is rather awkward, isn't it."

"Awkward? This is awkward? That's what you've got to say? 'This is awkward.' "

"Sorry about all that back in Stone Coal," Paul continued. "How did you find me?"

"You arrogant piece of shit." My voice was rising. "You think I was trying to find you? I couldn't care less about you, or where you came from, or where you went."

"So I guess it's CB you're looking for."

"Yeah. I guess so, but it was a big mistake on my part. I don't want to see you or 'CB,' as you call him. I'm leaving." I turned and headed down the steps.

"Hold on a minute." Paul was right behind me. "Give me a chance to explain a few things."

In no time I was in my car, but Paul had followed and was in the passenger side.

"You can't just leave," he said.

"Yep, I can. I just got here and I can just get gone, so if you'll get out of my car, I'm going to do just that."

"I'm not getting out Lewis Ray," he said.

"Well then, I guess you'll be going back to Stone Coal because that's where this car is headed."

We sat in silence, me staring straight ahead and Paul staring at me.

"I'm not getting out, Lewis Ray," Paul said firmly. "We have to talk. CB won't be home until tomorrow, it's late in the day, so you should just stay here. I don't know what you know or what you think you know, but let's sort this out, once and for all. And by the way, it's Paul Jacobs, not Jenkins. Same as your last name."

"I know. I overheard you and Mamma Lou talking in your apartment that night. I know CB is your dad and I know Mamma Lou is your mom."

"Wait," Paul interrupted. "Did Lou tell you that?"

"She didn't have to. I figured it out."

"Well you figured wrong. You got part of it right, though."

"Then why were you talking to Mamma Lou the other night?"

"There's a lot more to the story. Things I knew bits and pieces about, but I knew Lou would be able to fill in some blanks," Paul continued.

"Who is your mother?" I looked Paul squarely in the eyes.

"That's where it gets complicated. There is so much more you need to know, Lewis Ray. Let's go inside, get a bite to eat, and I'll tell you everything, or at least everything I know."

CHAPTER TWELVE

July 24, 1987

I glanced at my watch as Gracie moved her chair in closer to mine.

"Honey, you got plenty of time. I won't rattle on long enough to make you late." Gracie smiled and patted my hand.

"As I was saying," Gracie continued, "there were lots of rumors and some speculation going around. It pretty much died down years ago, but it has started to stir again this week. It's none of it my business, but I guess if they's a chance it might hurt or embarrass you I'll make it my business."

"Okay Gracie, as you say let's split the baccer patch wide open." I settled back in my chair. "That summer of my senior year when Paul showed up, I had lots of questions. I drove all the way to Russell, Kentucky, which at the time seemed like a journey across the country, and I tracked down my father. I had no idea what I was in for or what all I was going to find out on that trip. But I found out a lot . . . a whole lot. Gracie, you say that the rumors that are flying around may hurt or embarrass me. What do you mean by that?"

Gracie hesitated and rubbed her chin with her with arthritic fingers.

"What exactly did your daddy tell you those many years ago?"

※ ※ ※

September 8, 1967

CB's Narrative

After leaving Stone Coal, I traveled from pillar to post, working odd jobs and living from one half-pint of bootleg Old Crow to the next. I ended up in Grundy, Virginia, for a while, where a good man by the name of Javier gave me a hand up. Javier was a Mexican immigrant, better known as a wetback at the time. He had a small welding shop and he allowed me to live in the back room. In return for a minimal salary and a roof over my head, I worked for him and learned his trade. His rules were simple. I had to stay sober and treat his customers with respect. Though his English was pretty good, his accent was thick and he often got his gender pronouns wrong; he as she and vice versa. People could be cruel to foreigners, especially ones with darker skin. Javier admitted that it was very hard being a spick amongst a bunch of hillbillies, so he learned early to keep his head down, do good work, and treat his customers well. He expected no less of me.

Javier had a daughter, Rosita, who was my same age. She came to the shop most every afternoon and did the books for Javier. She was a beautiful Latina, with flowing black hair, big brown eyes, and a personality much like Javier's—quiet, polite and stick-to-business. I was immediately taken by Rosita and looked forward to her daily visits to the shop. I paid her all the attention she would allow.

I had remained sober for over a year, for the most part. I had my occasional fall from grace, but never let Javier see me drunk and was always at work at the appointed time. By all appearances I had tamed the beasts of my past.

Rosita eventually succumbed to my pursuits, and by the next summer we had rented a small house not too far from Javier's shop. We told Javier that we had gotten married in a neighboring town, but in truth I was not divorced from Lou, as far as I knew. Several years later I learned that she had obtained a divorce in my absence, based upon abandonment.

I had always planned to reconnect with my children, but it seemed the longer it went the harder it became to do so, and the easier it became to let that part of my life remain closed off.

Rosita and I were trying to make a life for ourselves. I was still working at the shop with Javier, and Rosita had picked up a few additional small businesses to do the books for. I was outperforming anything I had ever done before in my life, but the occasional weekend binges continued.

Suffice it to say, it came as quite a shock that morning when Paul was dropped at my doorstep. He was a scared eleven-year-old boy with black hair, pale complexion, and eyes as hollow as empty bowls. I had spent a summer in Alton, West Virginia, when I was only seventeen. My father, long divorced from my mom, worked for the Kentucky West Virginia Gas Company and had landed me a summer job cutting weeds along the company right-of-ways. The work was hard and hot, but I was young and eager. The other boys on the weed crew were older than I and we were all housed at the company barracks. It was there that I developed my taste for cheap whiskey. I also came to know a girl, Brenda Jenkins, who lived down the street from the barracks and was two years my senior. Although she didn't technically steal my virginity, she became the first that was more than a quick "thank you ma'am."

So on that morning, Brenda, saying she could no longer care for our child, who up until that moment I didn't know existed, left Paul with me. Rosita was more understanding than I could ever have asked anyone to be. She and Paul and I attempted to make a family, and did pretty good for a time, but old demons came back to haunt me and before long my drinking and carousing had overtaken my life again. I began to show up at the shop drunk, or miss work altogether. Javier had no choice but to let me go, and in all truth, Rosita had no choice but to go back home to Javier and her mother. I was not much of a mate or a father.

For the next several years I wandered around the area, Paul in tow sometimes and sometimes back with his mother. I picked up a few welding jobs along the way, losing them just as quickly and moving on. Brenda would take Paul for spells, but her life was not much, if any, more stable than mine, so he ended up being shuffled back and forth his entire adolescence. As I said, I wasn't much of a father. I reasoned that Lewis Ray and Annie had Lou and I had so very little to offer, so I just stayed away.

Somehow Paul made it through. Sobriety was and is an elusive goal for me. I know the twelve steps backwards and forwards and have been to more AA meetings than I can count. Sometimes I think I have this thing conquered, but just as often I find myself back in the familiar glow of dim bar lights, taking comfort in a glass of bourbon. I've been sober now for seven months, not the longest I've ever made it, but maybe this time it's going to stick.

Maybe.

⁂

July 24, 1987

Gracie sighed and rubbed her forehead with her blue-veined hands.

"Well, like I said," Gracie continued, "there were lots of rumors at the time. But rumors in Stone Coal are like leftover cornbread. They get old and they dry up, and people look for something fresh. Time goes on and new gossip takes the place of old scandals. What's become of your father?"

"I never saw him after that day in Russell. I hear from Paul occasionally. As I understand, my dad died about ten years ago. He never really slipped the collar of addiction, but Paul said he had been sober for a few months before his death. Unfortunately, the damage had been done. As an adult, I never knew my dad so I didn't grieve his death, except maybe in some obligatory way. I grieved instead for not knowing him for most of my life, but I never mourned the person. I was only around eight years old when he left, so I never knew the person."

"Once you knew your daddy's story what did you do with all that? That's a big old bag of rocks for a teenager to haul around."

"It's hard to say. Mamma Lou and I never discussed it."

"Did you ever tell Travis about what all your daddy told you?"

"Eventually . . ."

CHAPTER THIRTEEN

September 9, 1967

The carnival grounds were all but deserted. Deep ruts were left in the sodded field where the heavy tractor trailers had pulled out after a pre-dawn rain. Without the midway and the sideshows and rides as landmarks, I had no idea where Kissimmee's trailer had been, but as I surveyed the remaining few campers it became obvious she had already left. I approached a larger Airstream, larger than Kissimmee's, and tapped lightly on the silver door. No answer. I tapped again, this time with a bit more force.

"I'm not home," someone yelled from behind me. It was Lola la Farge, tiptoeing gingerly across the field, taking care to avoid the standing water in the muddy tracks. As she got nearer, I observed that the harsh light of day was no friend to an aging stripper.

"Where'd the carnival go?"

"A lot of them are headed for Logan over in West Virginia. As you can see, most everyone's already gone. Myself, I'm going to Florida for a few months. My season is over."

"How about the guessing girl? Do you know if she went to Logan?"

"Honey, I don't even know her name. I'm not a carney, I'm a performing artist. I don't mix much with the carneys."

"Yep," I said, "I saw the barker advertising your show a couple of nights ago."

"I guess that means you didn't pay and come in."

"No, I am a little tight on money right now, but it looked like a good show."

"It's a great show, dearie. Great." Lola continued as she jangled her keys and unlocked her trailer door.

"Used to be I played some of the biggest clubs in the country: Chicago, Vegas, you name it, dearie. Was even with a troupe that did a stint across the big pond in the forties. Oh well, now it's just me and Teddy. Teddy's my fiancé. He's also my agent. He does all the promotion, booking, and he emcees the show. He'll be back in a few and we'll hook up the trailer and head to Ocala."

"If I were wanting to locate the guessing girl, how would I find out where she might be?" I was hoping Miss LaFarge might be of some help, despite her insistence that she was not a carney.

"The season is definitely winding down. She may have gone to Logan with the rest, but a lot of the carneys start making their way south about now. Anyhoo, if she works mainly with Farber Brothers, their office is in Kissimmee, Florida. Hang on a minute. I think I have one of Manny's cards. Manny's not a Farber and he's not a brother, but he . . . hang on."

Lola disappeared into the silver trailer and momentarily emerged, business card in hand.

"Here you go, dearie." She handed me Manny's card.

Manuel Spurlock

Owner-Operator

Farber Bros. Shows

Fun for the Entire Family

Box 4115, Kissimmee, Fla. Tel: Wilson 63411

Soon I was back on the highway, taking stock of my situation. I had left home three days ago, picnicked with a hooker at a roadside park, smoked weed for the first time, fought with a brother I never knew I had, met up with my long-lost father, and now I was looking for a girl who travels with the carnival and whose name I don't even know.

As I crossed the river into West Virginia, State Route 23 came to a split. Right would lead me back to Kentucky and Stone Coal; left to Logan, West Virginia.

CHAPTER FOURTEEN

Monday morning found me in Principal Gordon's office going through the prescribed procedure for re-admittance to school, a forged note from Mamma Lou in hand.

"Mr. Jacobs, have you taken time to reflect on the incident that resulted in your suspension?" Mr. Gordon was as stern and formal as a prison warden.

"Yes sir."

"And what have you learned?"

"That I should not fight at school," I said rather dismissively.

"So that's the best you can come up with?" Mr. Gordon stared just above my head, seemingly fixed on a point out the window. "That and a bogus note from your mother? Lewis Ray, I'm not going to mince words here. I realize that this note is some concoction that you and probably a friend came up with, but knowing your mother I'm far from astonished. As I'm sure you are aware, I was the principal here when she was a student. I am left to assume that either she is not aware of your suspension, or simply doesn't care. I must say that your tenure here has been much less remarkable than that of your mother. Surprisingly, until this incident, you have managed to turn in three acceptable years, no small feat given the lack of parental support you have received. Now you are embarking on the last year of your high school education." Mr. Gordon paused. "I've seen many young people, especially those with backgrounds similar to yours, take a downward spiral just as it appeared they may defy the odds and actually succeed. Don't join those ranks," he continued patronizingly. "I'm willing to grant you grace on this one occasion. Do you understand the meaning of grace, son? It is that which is granted to you through absolutely no doing or merit of your own. A gift. So now go back to class and don't darken my doorway for the remainder of this school year."

I headed for the door as fast as my feet would carry me.

"Mr. Jacobs, don't squander this opportunity. It will not unfold this way ever again. Understand?"

"Yes sir."

After school that day I drove by Travis's house, but once again did not stop. Instead I drove back to Bosco and parked in the alley across from the entrance to Frog's. Looking through the rearview mirror the words "mooR looP" stared back at me from a small weathered sign over the basement-level door. Frog was racking a game of nine-ball for a couple of older guys when I entered. The outside light cut a swath across the windowless room and all eyes turned to me. A hand-lettered sign, *"Be 18 or Be Gone,"* hung alongside a yellowed

1962 pinup calendar that depicted a naked woman astraddle a pool cue, posed in the same manner as a witch riding a broom.

Frog was a slightly built man and probably much younger than his appearance would have you believe. His skin was darkened, most likely by some genetic hiccup in his background; it was certainly not by the sun, for he seldom saw the light of day. Frog had run the pool-room for as long as I could remember.

"Hey, Lewis Ray." Frog hung the rack on a worn wooden peg, one of six that corresponded to each of the green felt-topped tables in the narrow room. "What brings you in? Taking up pool?"

"Not hardly, Frog. These guys would fleece me in a heartbeat." At Frog's, betting was as much of an art as was the skill of the game.

"Frog, could I talk to you a minute?" I asked, nodding toward the back room that Frog used for his office and for storage space.

I followed Frog, weaving between tables and pausing to allow patrons to complete their shots.

"Whatcha need'n?" Frog asked as he sat on his small wooden desk, one end of which was propped up with cinder blocks.

"If I wanted to buy some grass, uh, marijuana, do you think you could help me find some?"

It was well known that Frog was Bosco's supplier of pot, but, naive as I was, I knew better than to ask him outright.

"I might could." Frog wiped his mouth with a stained handkerchief he pulled from his hip pocket. "I don't sell it myself, mind you, but I might know somebody who does. What do you want, a nickel bag?"

"A nickel bag?" I repeated the question.

"A five-dollar bag. About a quarter ouzie. Or I can get you a lid for fifteen."

"A nickel's worth will be good."

Frog slapped his leg and let out a cackle, which in turn induced a coughing fit.

"A nickel's worth?" Frog asked between coughs and laughs. "You mean a nickel bag. Boy, if you're going to smoke it you got to learn to talk it. I'll see if I can get a hold of that feller who sells it. You come back tonight right after I close."

※ ※ ※

The nights were beginning to usher in the chill of the changing season and I pulled my jacket close as I sat on the rock and took one last drag. It was the first joint I had ever rolled and it bore no resemblance to Kissimmee's. It wasn't smooth and neat like hers, but even so the pleasant aftereffects felt much the same. I lay back on the rock and stared at the night sky.

"I thought I'd find you here." It was Travis.

"How did you get here? It's pitch dark. I didn't hear a car."

"Bat sonar, remember?" Travis laughed as he eased himself down beside of me.

"I drove by your house today . . . and last week . . . and the week before that. Kind of pathetic ain't it."

I could hardly make Travis out in the dim light of the ten-cent moon, but I could see that he had a black patch over his left eye.

"I would say why didn't you stop, but I know better. I don't need any lecture to know what a shit I was at the hospital." Travis turned his head at an angle to bring me into his field of vision.

"No big deal," I said.

"Aren't you going to comment on my new look? I think I look like a one-eyed hombre in a Clint Eastwood movie. What do you think?"

"I was thinking more like Long John Silver, if you just had a peg leg and a parrot on your shoulder."

"Touché." Travis laughed. I breathed easier.

"Hey," Travis continued, "did I smell reefer when I was walking up the path? Or were you smoking corn silks or rabbit tobacco?"

"I hope you're better at rolling than I am." I handed Travis what I had come to know as my nickel bag, and a pack of OCBs.

Pretty soon Travis and I were lying back on the rock staring into the night sky.

"You know," Travis broke the silence, "south of the equator the night sky looks entirely different. See the Big Dipper?" Travis pointed skyward. "In Africa they can't even see it and in northern Australia they can see it, but it's upside down. And they have the Southern Cross, which points straight to the south pole. Doesn't the Southern Cross sound so much more beautiful than a dipper? And the North Star? It's probably the South Star in South America."

"Travis, do you just make this shit up?" I asked. "I don't know the North Star from your anus. Your anus Travis . . . Uranus. Get it?"

"Yep, I get it, Lewis Ray. I'm half-blind, not half-stupid."

We were quiet again, neither of us saying it, but both of us perhaps feeling as if we were up looking down.

"Travis?"

"Yeah buddy." Travis was still staring into the sky.

"I saw my dad this weekend."

"That's what I heard."

"And Paul. I saw him too. He lives with dear ole dad."

"Yep, heard that too."

"Well shit, is there anything you don't know?"

"Not much, Lewis Ray. This is Stone Coal, you know. One person farts and half the town smells it."

"What do you know about Linda Hudson?" I asked.

"You really want to know?" Travis lifted his head from the rock and squinted with his one eye.

"Guess I must or I wouldn't have asked."

"Well, I know she's pretty. I know she's very different. She's intriguing in an odd sort of way. I know she's smart. I know she's reckless. I know she's your girlfriend."

"My girlfriend?" I interrupted. "What are we, in the fourth grade?"

"Uh," Travis continued, "I know that you were sleeping with her and I know that after my accident I started sleeping with her too. I know that it was a fucked-up thing to do to a friend. I know that she doesn't deserve someone like you, and I know that I probably don't either."

"Okay."

"Okay? Is that all you're going to say, Lewis Ray? Okay?"

I thought for a while.

"Yep, okay."

CHAPTER FIFTEEN

Travis and I knew our lives would forever be connected about four years before old Jonathan's wake. It was a night we never spoke of again. Never.

Ada Wicker, Travis's mother, was everything that Mamma Lou was not. She was quiet, self-contained, a deep thinker, and a homebody. She hardly wore any makeup, and even as an eight-year-old kid, I thought she was beautiful. Maybe it was because she was so different from Mamma, but I always enjoyed spending time at Travis's house. Ada's husband, Eldon, worked night shift in the mines and he and my father were drinking buddies. Most mornings when they got off work they drank their way home. That was, until my father got laid off.

It was an early spring night; one of those where only the long low moan of the bullfrogs shushed the chirping of the field crickets. I was staying over at Travis's house. Ada had fixed us a supper of spaghetti and meatballs with buttered light bread, and rice pudding for dessert.

After supper Ada sat in her favorite chair, legs crossed and feet curled and tucked up under her. In one hand she held a paperback folded at the spine, and in the other a Pall Mall. She was lost in her story, and Travis and I were sprawled on the floor working a jigsaw puzzle that we had worked many times before. We were complaining that there was nothing to do in Stone Coal on such a nice night.

So on that spring night that Travis and I never spoke of again, Ada went to bed at around ten o'clock. Bidding us goodnight, she gave us a stern admonition not to leave the house, and then went down the hall to the room she and Eldon shared.

Likewise, Travis and I soon went off to his room, and lay across the bed just staring out the open window. We contemplated sneaking out but decided there was really nothing fun that two eight-year-old boys could get into in Stone Coal that late at night. We talked and told stories—who was the prettiest girl in our grade; what high schooler would we like best to see naked; and which one of us would likely be the first to get laid. Travis started to yawn, and finally in mid-sentence he lay his head on the flabby pillow we were to share and fell asleep. I continued to stare out the window watching the occasional headlights pass on Route 80, which paralleled the cornfield below the Wickers' home. In time I guess I must have fallen asleep as well. I don't know if it was instinct or the noise that awakened me, or perhaps both, but when I came to I was confused and disoriented. But not for long.

Anyone who lives in a coal town knows the sound of the mine siren. Each Friday at noon—noon sharp, not 11:59 or 12:01, but at noon—the siren is tested. It begins as a low agonizing groan that builds to a mournful hum and then to a dreadful and unnerving scream. Each Friday at noon, for one full minute, the town is reminded of how perilous mining is and of how temporary life as we know it can be in a coal camp. And then sixty seconds later as the siren wanes and dies, the coal cars rumble down the track, customers at the Whip 'n Sip polish off their lunch specials, and Uncle Wallace fills another tank at the Phillips 66.

The siren was in full scream mode when I sat bolt upright in bed. Travis was already at the window.

"My God, Lewis Ray, there's trouble at the mine." Travis turned and ran for the door, me right behind him.

Travis swung the door wide open and directly across the narrow hall and squarely in our faces, was Ada Wicker, her bare white breasts swinging from side to side as she fumbled to pull her blouse together. And just behind her, hopping and stumbling with one pants leg on, his flaccid penis bobbing up and down amidst a nest of curly black hair, was my father, CB Jacobs.

It was not until years later that I was able to fully comprehend the impact of that incident, and to have actual words for the humiliation and visceral sense of loss and betrayal that I felt. Realizing my father and my best friend's mother were having sex in the next room confirmed in my mind, even at that young age, that we were indeed white trash.

"You've got to take me to the mine. Now!" Ada pulled one of Travis's sweatshirts over her head.

"We can't go there together. You know that."

"All I know is my husband is in that mine and I have to get there and you have to take me. I don't give a damn what people will say."

They disappeared out the back door as if Travis and I were invisible.

Thirty minutes later Travis and I arrived at the mine on our bikes. It appeared that most of Stone Coal was already gathered there. The mine entrance was brightly illuminated with portable spotlights which were mounted on aluminum poles and powered by gasoline generators that belched and sputtered. Travis and I climbed atop the powder house where we had full vista of the pandemonium that was erupting. Family members were frantically searching amongst the black-faced miners who were coughing and wheezing, some lying on the ground and many crouched, hands on knees, struggling to suck in clean air.

"Have you seen my son? Have you seen my brother? Have you seen my husband?" And occasionally, there was the joyous yet still disturbing wail of relief.

Melvin Hicks, the mine foreman, was speaking into a bullhorn as he made his way through the assembly.

"Miners, please tag out. Please retrieve your pit tag from the work board. We need to make sure everyone is out of the mine. Please miners, you must brass out immediately." His amplified voice was ringing and echoing off the high cliffs surrounding the scoop entrance.

"Please, miners, you must brass out." Melvin walked in circles repeating the plea over and over.

Every miner going underground was required to hang his brass ID marker, known as a pit tag, on a hook on the work board as he entered the mine. The miner's number and name were embossed on the tag, and the foreman could see who was in the mine at any given time by glancing at the board. And at the change of shift new tags went up on the corresponding shift board and old tags came down as coal-dust-laden miners, empty dinner buckets in hand, snuffed their carbide lights and headed for home.

Slowly the work board began to empty as miners approached one by one and removed their tags.

"Melvin, I got Daddy's tag," a young boy called. "He's over by the truck. He's okay, just winded."

Melvin nodded.

"Every miner must tag out immediately." The drone continued.

When no miners were left in line, the sad realization settled in that there were still tags hanging on the board. Melvin approached the work station. A dead silence hung heavy in the air as Melvin lay the bullhorn on the ground beside him.

"There are five tags left on the board. I will read the names. If you are present or if you have seen these miners, please let me know now. First, Denny Bentley, Denny Bentley."

A shriek of grief pierced the silence as Denny's wife, Loraine, fell to the ground. Soon surrounded by family and friends, her sobs were muffled as Melvin retrieved the next tag from the board.

"Forrest Conley, Forrest Conley."

Another agonizing wail . . . and then another.

"I haven't seen my dad." Travis edged closer to the eave of the powder house.

"He's out there, I bet." I didn't know what else to say.

"No he's not," Travis said. "I know he's not. And it's my mom's fault."

"Jimmy Slone. Jimmy Slone," Melvin read from the tag.

"Here Melvin," came a weakened voice, "I'm here."

Jimmy was leaned up against a pickup truck, his blackened face streaked from tears of joy or sadness or maybe from the sting of mine gas.

There was only one more tag on the board. Travis dug his fingernails into my forearm; his eyes were clenched closed. I took his other hand in mine and held it tightly.

"Eldon Wicker."

He only said it once, for a gasp and guttural moan came from across the crowd. Ada Wicker buried her face in my father's chest as he put his arms around her stooped shoulders and pulled her close.

Mamma Lou stepped out from the crowd and glared coldly at the two of them, then turned and left.

It was three days before the four bodies were recovered from the mine face and another three before the funerals. Mamma Lou never made mention of the incident and we never went to the visitations or took over food, or did any of the things small-town people do when neighbors die.

My father boarded a Trailways bus and left Stone Coal for good the night of the mine disaster.

CHAPTER SIXTEEN

Selective Service System
ORDER TO REPORT FOR
ARMED FORCES PHYSICAL EXAMINATION

Lewis Ray Jacobs
116 South Hwy 80
Stone Coal, KY 14697

March 6, 1968

Selective Service No.
36 9 50 878
You are hereby directed to present yourself for Armed
Forces Physical Examination by reporting to:
Assembly Room
8th Floor Federal Building
1060 Liberty Avenue
Ashland, KY 40897
on:
April 5, 1968
at:
7:00 A.M.
Please contact your local Selective Service Board for
instruction on where and at what time to report locally
for transportation to the regional induction center
cited above.

Sincerely,
Thomas Gallent
Secretary of Regional Board

Selective Service System
ORDER TO REPORT FOR
ARMED FORCES PHYSICAL EXAMINATION

Travis Eldon Wicker
860 South Hwy 80
Stone Coal, KY 14697

March 6, 1968

Selective Service No.
36 8 55 656
You are hereby directed to present yourself for Armed
Forces Physical Examination by reporting to:
Assembly Room
8th Floor Federal Building
1060 Liberty Avenue
Ashland, KY 40897
on:
April 5, 1968
at:
7:00 A.M.
Please contact your local Selective Service Board for
instruction on where and at what time to report locally
for transportation to the regional induction center
cited above.

Sincerely,
Thomas Gallent
Secretary of Regional Board

CHAPTER SEVENTEEN

Travis and I, on the same day, received our orders to report for our physicals. News that Travis had been called up was met with both outrage and amusement by our friends. I picked him up at 3:30 AM on the morning of April 5 and we made our way to the Dixie Drive-In in Mill Creek where a chartered Greyhound was waiting in the parking lot, diesel engine humming, ready to get us to Ashland by 7:00 AM. The bus was nearly full when we arrived. I boarded first and Travis bounded up the steps behind me. Applause and laughter greeted him as Travis shouldered a make-believe rifle, closed his right eye, and pretended to stare down the sights with his patched left eye. After firing a few imaginary rounds, the recoil taking him back a step and causing his gun to rise in the air, Travis shouted, "I'm hoping for sharpshooter, whatda yall think?"

Good-natured pats on the back and head rubs ushered Travis down the aisle of the Greyhound and he and I settled in a seat near the rear.

"Four o'clock sharp." The driver gazed up in the mirror at the load of boys behind him. "Wheels are rolling."

And with that, a hiss, swish, and thud closed the big door. The driver dimmed the interior lights and the bus eased forward.

The morning sun awakened me, and for the second time in the last seven months I was welcomed to Ashland by the foundries' tall smokestacks spewing white steam skyward. Travis's head was on my shoulder, his neck bent at an unnatural angle, his mouth wide open, and his breaths coming in noisy snorts. I shrugged my shoulder, lightly at first and then with more purpose, until Travis slowly opened his one eye and looked around the bus.

"Shit, my neck is breaking." Travis sat upright and rubbed and massaged the muscles of his shoulders and neck. "Don't think a pinched nerve in my spine will keep me out of the draft do you, Lewis Ray?"

"A one-eyed sniper with a bad neck? I don't know, Travis."

The bus winded its way through the narrow streets of downtown Ashland. Most of the boys were awake now and conversations were becoming more hushed. A palpable tension had replaced the lighthearted banter of just two hours ago. Finally, the Greyhound was directed through a big open gate in a chain-link fence and signaled to park alongside at least twelve other buses exactly like ours. We looked out on wide-eyed young men, papers in hand, standing single file at the side entrance of the building. Some of us began to get to our feet.

"Hold your horses, boys," the driver called out. "Sarge'll be here in a minute to give you instruction. I'm heading to the drivers' lounge. I'm about to piss like a gray mule on a flat rock. I'll see yall this afternoon."

Johnny Frank got off the bus and stood by the door, fumbling for his cigarettes and lighter.

"Recruit! Who told you to get off the bus?"

It was a slightly built young man, not much older than us, buzzed head, clipboard in hand, and a manila folder tucked under his arm.

"I just thought I'd have a smoke." Johnny put his cigarettes back into his breast pocket.

"From now on you will smoke, eat, piss, shit, and cry for your mamma when I tell you to. Capeesh?" Johnny nodded. "Until you get back on this bus this afternoon, your ass belongs to the U.S. Armed Forces. Now back on the bus and in your seat, recruit."

Johnny hurried back on the bus and took his seat, the young officer at his heels.

"Recruits, I am Staff Sergeant Robert Glass. You are here because you have been selected by your country or else you have volunteered to be considered for active military service. All recruits must be evaluated for physical and mental suitability, and that is the purpose of your being here today. You will be told exactly what you need to know when you need to know it. There are over two hundred and fifty recruits being processed today, so do not impede the process by asking superfluous questions. If you truly do not understand or hear the instructions, they will be repeated. I have in my hand a stack of papers. Each set of papers has a number at the top. This will be your number for the day. Everything you do will be tied to this number and you will be processed in numerical order, that is, number 341 will be followed by 342, and so forth. Now as you get off of the bus, I will hand you a packet. Please proceed to the side door where you will enter a room furnished with long tables. There are ample pencils on each table. Complete the first and second pages of the paperwork and you will be given further instructions at that point."

I followed Travis off of the bus and received packet number 1147.

"What's your number?" I asked lowly over Travis's shoulder.

"One less than yours, dumbass."

Although that made total sense, I needed some reassurance. After filling out the first two pages, which consisted of predictable demographic information, we sat in silence—about fifty of us—until we were called to the front in groups of ten. We were then directed into the adjacent room where, one at a time, we were instructed to approach a small gray desk, behind which sat a thin, wiry woman whose hair was pulled so tight in a bun that she could have passed for Asian. She was obviously a civilian since she was not in uniform. Black half-glasses, from which she seldom looked up, rested low on her nose.

As Travis approached the table, Tight Bun extended her right hand and made fluttering motions with her pale bony fingers. Travis correctly assumed that she was asking for his papers, which she silently took from him and flipped to the third page.

"Are there any physical, emotional, or mental impairments that you deem would render you unsuitable to serve in the United States Armed Forces?" She did not look up.

"Are you kidding me?" Travis squinted his one eye.

"Are there any physical, emotional, or mental impairments that you deem would render you unsuitable to serve in the United States Armed Forces?" This time she looked Travis squarely in the face.

"You are kidding me, right?"

"Are there any physical, emotion . . ."

"Lady, I got one friggin eye."

Tight Bun went back to Travis's papers and checked a couple of boxes.

"Do you have any documentation from a qualified practitioner to substantiate your assertion that you are not physically, emotionally, or mentally suited to serve in the United States Armed Forces?"

With that Travis bent down until he was nearly nose to nose with the pale-faced woman and he flipped up the black patch covering his left eye.

Tight Bun recoiled momentarily, but just as quickly regained her composure and chose a stamp from a tree of rubber stamps on her desk, thumped it once in a red ink pad, and made three firm whops on the page.

"Hallway to the left please."

It was my turn now, and, as was her procedure, without looking up the woman fluttered her fingers and took my papers.

"Do you have any physical . . ."

"No."

"Hallway to the right please."

It was nearly three o'clock before I got back to the bus. I had been poked and prodded from head to toe and my balls had been cupped in the hands of another man. Someone had looked down my throat and in my ears, and had stuck their finger up my ass. I had taken a test that a third-grader could easily pass and had been questioned about my mental stability, criminal background, and sexual preference. I had been queried about any subversive activities and acts of moral turpitude that I may have been a part of. And at the end of it all it was determined that I was just what the United States Armed Forces was looking for. My 1-S deferment would be changed to 1-A on May 9, 1968, the date of my graduation from high school.

I saw Travis curled up asleep in our two seats as I made my way down the aisle. By this time the bus was near full again.

"1-A all the way!" Johnny Frank shook his fist over his head as I passed. "How 'bout you Lewis Ray?"

"Yep, me too," I said, with much less enthusiasm.

Travis woke up and scooted to the window seat.

"4-F here," Travis said. "No surprise. Poor old Romey Nobel is 4-F too. Couldn't pass the mental exam. I guess I'm in good company."

Romey sat across the aisle, dejected, with his head in his hands.

"Looks like I'm good to go," I said, trying not to show the angst that had settled in my gut ever since the tight-bunned woman—who was the first and ended up being the last of my encounters of the day—had stamped my papers with a bold, black ***Approved for Induction***. Not once, not twice, but three times, each stamp driving home the point.

Travis and I didn't talk much on the way home. A few of the boys, like Johnny Frank, were excited and seemingly couldn't wait to get called up. Several, like Romey, seemed to be embarrassed that, for whatever reason, they did not meet the qualifications. The vast majority were like me, staring at the floor, wondering if indeed in a few short months we would be transported to the mosquito-infested jungles of Southeast Asia.

And then there was Travis, trying his best to stay above the fray, knowing coming in that the horrible event that scarred his face and robbed him of his sight had made this day irrelevant. I wondered if he viewed that in any way a consolation, but I never asked.

The sun was almost setting as we arrived at the Dixie. Travis offered to spring for some beers at the Blue Star, but I just wanted to go home. Annie and Jerry were about to leave when I got to the trailer.

"How did it go?" Annie asked.

"I guess okay. It seems I'm fit as a fiddle."

"You want to talk about it? We're going to run down to P-burg to get a pizza at the Black Cat. Come with us."

"No," I said, "but thanks for the offer."

With that Annie and Jerry headed toward Prestonsburg and I headed for the rock.

CHAPTER EIGHTEEN

Selective Service System
ORDER TO REPORT FOR INDUCTION

The President of the United States

Lewis Ray Jacobs
116 South Hwy 80
Stone Coal, KY 14697

April 22, 1968

Selective Service No.
36 9 50 878
Greetings:
You are hereby ordered for induction into the Armed Forces of the United States and are to report to:
Assembly Room
8th Floor Federal Building
1060 Liberty Avenue
Ashland, KY 40897
on:
May 16, 1968
at:
8:00 A.M.
for forwarding to an Armed Forces Induction Station.

Sincerely,
Thomas Gallent
Secretary of Regional Board

CHAPTER NINETEEN

The night before I was to ship out, as the saying goes, though in fact I was shipping all the way to Missouri for basics, I picked Travis up at his home just at dusk. It was another spring evening and had much the same feel as that fateful spring evening of ten years ago. Though we often talked of the singular event that had thrust our small town into the national spotlight, albeit briefly, and had made the name Stone Coal synonymous with the death of four coal miners, Travis and I had yet to speak of the personal humiliation that had coincided with the event.

We stopped by the Blue Star and picked up a sack of Tall Boys, for which Dakey refused payment.

"These are on me." Dakey's Lucky Strike bobbed up and down from its perpetual resting place in the corner of her painted red lips. "You be safe over there, Lewis Ray. I'll be praying for you."

Stone Coal in its entirety knew that me and Johnny Frank had both been called up and, barring some divine intervention, would end up in Vietnam in a few short weeks. My journey was to start at eight o'clock the next morning, at which time I was to report to the same Federal Building in Ashland where a month or so earlier it had been determined that I was fit to serve. From there the group of us would be bused to Charleston where we would board a plane for Fort Leonard Wood, an army base located in the heart of the Ozark Mountains. Just my luck, I thought, another podunk town in another hillbilly holler.

Just after Christmas Linda had disappeared from Stone Coal, reportedly moving to Ironton, Ohio, to live with her aunt and finish her senior year there. It seemed odd, but odd was Linda's normal. Travis and I, characteristically, had never spoken again of his betrayal with Linda. I let it go and let Linda go.

"Well, Lewis Ray, where to?"

"Don't much matter."

"Well it's your car and your gas, so it's your choice."

"Okay, let's start at the strip mine and go from there."

About forty-five minutes later we sat in the Comet, its nose pointing westward, sipping lukewarm sixteen-ounce Schlitz beers and overlooking the small cluster of lights below, which was Bosco.

"This feels just like sitting under the Hollywood sign doesn't it?" Travis said facetiously.

"I've never been to Hollywood, but I can't imagine it being more exciting than this," I said.

"Hey, I got an idea."

"Oh shit Travis. Not tonight. If I can just live til tomorrow without somebody getting snakebit or something . . ."

"Then what? You'll get to go to Vietnam and get your pecker shot off? Buddy, I hate to break it to you but you got nothing to lose. Anyway, all I was suggesting is that we go to Lothair to Cooley's. I know we aren't old enough, but they would never turn away a guy getting ready to go fight for the good old U. S. of A. Whatdayasay?"

"Not Cooley's, that's Mamma Lou's hangout. How about Club 80?"

"Club 80 it is. And guess what? The tab's on me tonight. Drink what you want. I got it."

We had already downed three Tall Boys each by the time we reached Club 80. The long windowless cinderblock building that looked so barren and seedy in the daylight took on a carnival-like atmosphere after dark, with neon lights bordering the eaves and a giant flashing yellow arrow atop the building beckoning passersby on highway eighty. Two smaller signs alternately flashed *Drinks* and *Eats*. As we weaved our way through the vehicles in the crowded parking lot, I made out the unmistakable sound of urine splattering on gravel. Three cars over, hanging on to the antenna of his Corvair with one hand and his penis with the other, Johnny Frank was listing side to side as he emptied his beer-filled bladder.

"Lewis Ray!" Johnny Frank yelled, letting go of the car temporarily, bobbing back and forth, and no doubt pissing down his leg, "Wyooooooo, Semper Fi mutha fucker. We're gonna give them gooks a good old hillbilly ass kicking ain't we?"

"Yeah, Johnny." I kept walking, muttering under my breath, "Semper Fi my ass . . . we're getting drafted into the friggin army. Idiot."

A short line had formed as we approached the pay window, behind which sat Lily Combs, wife of Mac Combs and co-owner of Club 80. IDs were shown and cover charges collected as patrons were handstamped and allowed to enter.

"Hang on a minute." Travis went ahead. He and Lily talked briefly, and soon Travis motioned for me to join them.

"Make a fist, sweetie." Lily smiled.

She stamped the back of my hand and then the back of Travis's.

"Thank you for what you're doin'. You take care over there."

Travis and I parted the beaded curtains and entered the big, dimly lit room. I had never been to Club 80 before. Actually I had never been to any nightclub before, save for Cooley's when I was summoned to come and get Mamma Lou one night. She had passed out on the commode in the ladies' room. Anne and Cooley Baker had helped load her in the back seat of the Comet.

"Travis, Lewis Ray . . . over here."

It was Patty Watts and Bunny Scott, two girls from Stone Coal who were a few years older than Travis and me. They scooted their chairs together, making room for us to join them.

"I hear you're shipping out, Lewis Ray." Bunny rubbed my shoulder.

The waitress, a woman with a French twist held in place by jeweled hair combs and stabbed through with a yellow number two pencil, approached our table.

"What'll the rest of yall have?" she asked, as she placed a highball in front of me.

"What's this?"

"Bourbon and Coke. It's from the bar."

I looked to the counter where sat a lone patron, Jack Martin, an older guy I knew from Stone Coal. Jack had just been discharged from the army, after completing two tours in Vietnam. As we made eye contact Jack raised his glass and nodded before returning his attention to the evening news on the small television screen over the bar.

AJ Campbell and the Greystones were tuning up and checking their sound levels as the room began to fill up. I had seldom danced, and it was widely regarded by my friends that I was no good at all at it, so I planned to just sit and blend in with the vinyl tablecloth.

The Greystones opened their first set with "Hello, I Love You" by The Doors.

"Come on, Lewis Ray."

Bunny hooked my arm with hers and led me to the center of the floor beneath the blueish cast of a long panel of blacklights. Our teeth took on the brilliance of Chicklets, and Bunny's pink blouse was as neon as the glass tubes that hung below the sagging eaves of Club 80.

The blacklights flickered off and were replaced by a flashing strobe that captured our movements in a series of snapshots.

When we got back to the table my nearly empty glass had been replaced with a full one. The hearty oaken flavor of top-shelf bourbon, a taste until that night foreign to me, mixed with the sweet and familiar Coca Cola made for a combination that I found all too appealing, and soon enough another empty glass was refilled, and then another.

By the time the band launched into their final song of the set, "Wild Thing," any reservations that I had ever had about my ability or desire to dance had long been lost to the bourbon, and I could feel my body jerking and swaying in rhythm with The Troggs.

As we made our way to the car at the end of the evening, shamefully, I found myself pissing in the parking lot before allowing Travis to drive us back toward Stone Coal.

"Hey buddy, we're going to stop at the Dixie and get some food and coffee in you."

I smushed my cheek against the passenger side window and gave thanks that the car was indeed moving, for sitting still invoked a very uncomfortable and nauseating spinning in my head.

Gracie had just turned off the lights when we arrived at the Dixie and had flipped the window sign from "Come in, We're Open" to "Sorry, We're Closed." Once she recognized her husband's old car she waved us to come on in.

"You'd better come and see Gracie before you head out of here. I'd a had a hissy fit if you left without saying goodbye." Gracie unlatched the door and showed us to a table in the corner.

"Lewis Ray here had a bit of bourbon and Coke tonight over at Club 80. You think you might find him a little sobering-up coffee?"

"Just turned the pot off, so it's still hot. Also I have a couple of slices of pee-can pie left."

Gracie disappeared into the kitchen and presently returned with pie and coffee for the both of us.

"It's this old gal's bedtime." Gracie smiled. "Just put those dishes in the sink and latch the front door behind you when yall leave. Lewis Ray . . . ," the tone shifted in Gracie's voice, "you're a good boy, and you stay good, you hear me? You be careful over there. I don't know why we're in that mess in the first place. You be sure and come back and see me when you're on furlough. You're one of my younguns now, and you too, Travis. You two have had a time, there's no doubt. But you've always leaned on each other and you always will. That's what buddies do."

With that Gracie bent over and planted a tender kiss in the crown of each our heads and turned and headed for the back door, using her apron to dab at her eyes.

"Travis," I said with a mouthful of pie.

"What?" Travis's mouth was equally full.

"I want you to have Tray."

"Tray. Your dog Tray?"

Tray was a bluetick who had wandered up to our trailer a few years back. Travis suggested we call him Old Dog Tray from the Stephen Foster ballad of the same name. Since I had never heard it, Travis sang the entire song to me ending with . . .

"He's gentle, he is kind;

I'll never, never find

A better friend than old dog Tray."

We agreed that Old Dog Tray was a suitable name, and even though he was my pet, Tray immediately took up with Travis.

"Yeah, I want you to have Tray."

"Old Dog Tray, the one that sleeps under my front porch?"

"Yeah, Old Dog Tray."

"Your dog Tray for whom my mother buys a fifty-pound bag of Big Red every month? Your dog Tray who has not been at your house for over two years? Your dog Tray who took up with me and has never left? You want me to take care of Tray, whom I have been taking care of ever since he wandered in."

"Well, I admit it's a technicality, but I'm trying to tie up some loose ends." I savored the last bit of Gracie's signature pecan pie.

"Done," Travis proclaimed resolutely. "Now let's get you to Stone Coal. We'll take a short nap on the rock and I'll deliver your sorry ass to Ashland by eight o'clock in the morning. Okay?"

"Okay."

CHAPTER TWENTY

It was much later in life that I came to realize the significance of the rock being the place Travis and I always retreated to. It was indeed our rock and our anchor. It was the one place where we sought sanctuary and found clarity, and it was exclusively ours. So it was entirely appropriate and predictable that in the hours before I would leave Stone Coal, perhaps for the last time, Travis and I would return to the rock.

The chill of the night had settled over the valley and I had retrieved a couple of army blankets I kept stowed under the trailer. Travis and I lay side by side, huddled under our blankets staring skyward, just as we had so many times before.

"It's hard to believe you're leaving Stone Coal, Lewis Ray."

"I always thought you'd be the one leaving and I'd be here holding down the fort. I guess Uncle Sam tricked us both."

"Uncle Sam and them damned Holy Rollers . . . I'm going to miss you, friend." Travis raised his head and propped it on his bent arm. "I promise I'll write you every day." Travis continued, "I won't do it, but I'll promise to. Actually I won't ever write to you."

"I promise not to read every letter you don't write. Deal?"

"Deal."

With that Travis yoked my head and gave me a light noogie. That's as close to sentimental as we ever got.

"In addition to Tray, I want you to have the Vomit."

"I can't take your car Lewis Ray. Let Annie drive it til you get back."

"Annie can't drive. You need a car, Travis, and God knows I won't have use for one for a long time. I went to the courthouse today. The papers are in the glove compartment."

"I can't take your car, Lewis Ray."

"It's done. You're going to drive me to Ashland in a few hours and then you and the Vomit are going to come back to Stone Coal and I'm going to go to Camp Whateverthefuck in Missouri and that's that."

Travis was silent for the longest time.

"Lewis Ray?"

"Yeah?"

"I think I'm going to cry my eye out."

At that we both laughed, and then fell silent again.

"Well, speaking of tying up loose ends," Travis broke the silence, "I guess you'll hear about it sooner or later, and I'd rather you hear it from me."

"Well that sounds serious."

"Well, yeah . . . uh, I heard from Linda Hudson a week or so ago. You know she lives in Ironton with her aunt."

"Yes, and?"

"Well it seems she is great with child, so to speak."

"Oh hell. You mean she went and got herself pregnant?"

"Not exactly. She got herself pregnant and then went. She's nearly ready to deliver. That's why she left Stone Coal over Christmas break."

Silence again for a period. It was I who asked the obvious question.

"Whose is it?"

"Well, you can do the math. It either belongs to you or me."

"What the hell, Travis? You or me? What's that supposed to mean?"

"It means what it means. She had been sleeping with both of us."

"And nobody else?"

"She says not."

"Do you believe her?"

Travis rubbed his forehead.

"Lewis Ray, it's not that I am defending Linda's veracity, but when she was sleeping with the both of us, everybody in Stone Coal knew it. If there had been another, don't you think everybody would have known that too?"

"Well what are we going to do?"

"I told her that I'd marry her."

"I'll marry her," I said with firmness.

"Lewis Ray, this isn't like calling dibs to ride shotgun. And besides, she said she didn't want to marry either one of us. She just thought we should know."

"What are we going to do, Travis?"

"Well, in a couple of hours I'm taking you to Ashland, and I'm going to come back to Stone Coal, and that's that."

"I can't just up and leave not knowing if we have fathered a child."

"Well it may be you or it may be me, but it ain't we, I can guarantee you that." Travis forced a laugh. "And besides, what are you going to do, call up Camp Whateverthefuck and say, well I'm sorry, I may have knocked up some girl, or maybe I didn't, but I can't show up for boot camp tomorrow. I'm really sorry."

"Shit, Travis. What a mess."

"Yep, it's a mess Lewis Ray. But you have no choice but to report for duty in a few hours, unless you would like to spend some time in a military prison. It is what it is and it will work itself out. Neither of us has any control over what Linda does. Hell, she may put it up for adoption, who knows. But if she wants anything from either of us she will have no problem whatsoever bringing it to us. Trouble will find you. You don't need to seek it out."

"So that's it? We just go on about our lives as if nothing has changed?"

"That's my plan, Lewis Ray. Now I'm ready to hear yours."

Somehow in the most difficult of situations, Travis always had the ability to say the words that made the most sense at the time. So as the darkest hour of night gave way to the earliest hint of dawn, I awoke Annie and Mamma Lou for a tearful goodbye, and Travis and I headed west on highway eighty.

Just before eight o'clock Travis poked me awake. For a split second it could have been any of a thousand mornings that Travis had poked me awake. But the fact that it wasn't stole my breath and stopped my heart.

"Well, soldier, here we are."

We were parked on the curb parallel to the chain-link fence that ran the perimeter of the induction center. A dozen or so young men, not all that much different than me, stood in groups, putting off that moment that they would enter the small gate, hand the sergeant their induction papers, and relinquish the life that they had known. Some were accompanied by weeping mothers, some by starry-eyed girlfriends, and others were stone-faced and alone.

"Travis," I said, thinking that there must be some words that would serve as an apt signature to mark this moment, but I was empty.

"Yeah?"

"Take good care, okay?"

"Okay."

I joined the short line on the sidewalk, waiting my turn to present my papers. I looked back over my shoulder and Travis had his hands at ten and two on the steering wheel of the Comet and his head was bowed at twelve.

That was the last time I ever saw Travis Wicker.

CHAPTER TWENTY-ONE

July 24, 1987

The business of burying the dead has evolved greatly in the mountains over the years. What used to be a three-day vigil in the home, just as old Jonathan's was those many years ago, has been replaced with practices more similar to those found in urban areas today. However, there is a certain feel to a mountain funeral that never changes, and it is like none other.

I was taken by an unsettling familiarity as I made my way through the gathering space just outside of the viewing rooms and the chapel at Slone's Funeral Home, a place I had not been in years. The passageway was lined with several small groups of older women. I could tell by their expressions they were wondering if I was someone they should know, and by their whispers as I passed that no . . . they couldn't place me. Overweight men in three-piece suits, carnations in their lapels and smelling salt ampules at the ready in their coat pockets, did the customary two-handed gesture, solemnly guiding the steady flow of mourners through the double doors to the chapel, indicating the service was about to begin.

I entered the big room, taking care not to look toward the open casket at the other end. As I was scanning the pews I saw my sister Annie making her way toward me, Jerry and their two boys at her side. We embraced and held each other tightly. Annie buried her face in my chest and I laid my head atop hers. We were both holding back tears, some for the sorrow at hand, and many for all the lost years.

"Boys, you remember your Uncle Lewis Ray." It was a statement not a question, and of course they did not, since they had only seen me a handful of times. But they politely nodded and extended their hands, confirming to me that Annie and Jerry had raised boys with manners and of good breeding. I would have expected no less.

"It's good to see you, Ray." Jerry hugged me. It was one of those half embraces that men do, but it was genuine.

Annie took me by the hand and led me down the center aisle, pausing about halfway. There on the end of the pew sat a woman I had not seen in nearly two decades.

"Your hair looks good Lewis Ray. Real nice."

"Thanks Mamma Lou, you look good too." And she did. My guess was that she was near sixty by now, but given her lifetime of age-fudging, I could not be sure. Her skirt was longer, her makeup more subtle, and her hair, though still blonde, had hints of gray. Either time or the soft wrinkles around her mouth and eyes had left her less harsh, and again I felt the pang of regret over the mislaid years.

I bent down to kiss Mamma on the forehead.

"Awful day for a funeral isn't it Lewis Ray," Mamma whispered. "Hotter'n shit out there."

Still holding Annie's hand, I felt her tug, and we made our way to the open casket. Annie pulled me to her, putting her arm around my waist and placing my arm over her shoulders.

I looked at the floor for the longest time, and then at the spray of death-red roses that covered the closed bottom half of the coffin. Eventually I allowed myself to look at the hands. I had never realized how identifying a person's hands could be. Although a little wrinkled and calloused by the years, paled by death and unnaturally colored by the embalming process, the square nails, the bold knuckles, and the long strong fingers were unmistakable; those were without a doubt the hands of Travis Wicker.

I must have allowed myself a glance to his face, for I have a vague memory of the black patch over his left eye and the tinge of gray at his temples. But what I remember most are his hands. Just as we were about to turn and leave, I reached into the casket, took Travis's hand into my own, and giving it a firm grasp I counted to five.

As Annie and I rejoined Jerry and the boys in a pew near the back, a tall, handsome, raven-haired young man was assisting a bent and broken Ada Wicker into the chapel. He gently led her to a reserved seat on the front pew, just steps away from the lifeless body of her son. He eased her down into her seat and slid his lanky frame in beside her, and Ada leaned into the embrace of her grandson.

I guess the service was good, or at least as good as a memorial service could be. I really don't remember much about it. I joined the motorcade to Stone Coal, but parked on a bluff overlooking the graveyard and watched as if it were a silent movie, void of voice, but rife with emotion.

✳ ✳ ✳

The trailer that I grew up in was long gone and the gravel drive was rutted and bare. I parked on the shoulder of Route 80 and made my way up the overgrown approach on foot. The spar grass that had taken root in the tracks was further indication that this property was long neglected, but the big rock still stood, just as it had those many years ago. The crippling heat of the day was starting to let up as I waded through the horseweed. Easing myself down, I took the folded sheets of lined notebook paper from my hip pocket: the pages worn and the creases rent, testament to the many times they had been pored over during the past few months. I again opened the letter and immersed myself in the bold cursive manuscript, a letter from Travis that had remained unanswered.

March 28, 1987

Dear Lewis Ray,

Well, old pal, I decided to break my promise of many years ago to not write to you. I hope you will do the same in not not reading my letter. I have often heard that true friends can pick right back up, even after years of being apart. I am sure that would be the case, but I doubt we get that opportunity. You see, my friend, the grim reaper has chosen to pick the low-hanging fruit, pun absolutely intended. What began as a nagging ache in my nut sack has bought me an express ticket to Beulah Land. I'm not all that eager to join the ranks of the dearly departed, but it appears the gig is nearly up. With that said, please don't come running to Stone Coal. I don't think you will. That's just not us.

I do have my sadness. Turner is more than I could ever have hoped for and it grieves me that I won't see what all he becomes. He was the only thing that Linda ended up being good for. She left just a few months after he was born and has had minimal contact over the years. If it had not been for my mother I don't know what I would have done. Just as dad's death gave her cause to go crazy as a shithouse rat, Turner gave her reason to return to the land of the sane again. I worry about her terribly and about how all of this will affect her. She swears she will be okay, and I hope that is the case.

Turner has lived under the shadow of the rumors, as have I. As soon as he was old enough to understand, we talked about it. I didn't want him to be blindsided by some cruel playground remark. We always made it a nonissue, because really, it didn't matter to us. They have tests these days, but neither of us want to know. We wouldn't do anything differently. He is a handsome devil, long and lanky like me, dark-haired like you. Sometimes a bit too quick to speak, but he has a sweet sensitivity that I have known in only one other soul on this earth.

So here comes the real reason for this letter. Lewis Ray, you must come to know Turner. He is a man in so many ways, but really, he's an eighteen-year-old kid who still needs someone like you to help him through the rough parts. When he falls, help him to his feet and get him back in the game. It should be easy enough—just continue being you. That is what I have used for guideposts these many years—if it were Lewis Ray, how would he handle it?

My biggest fear is that he won't make it out of these mountains. That godawful war of our day that took so many young lives, managed to deliver others out of the poverty and hopelessness of a world that as we knew it, has died. Stone Coal is now a shell. The Whip 'n Sip and the Blue Star are boarded up and the Phillips 66 burned to the ground by vandals. Frog has long graduated from selling a little weed to being a frontline distributor of pills and crack cocaine, insulating the top tier of a corrupt system. The kingpins are regular donors to the church and every Sunday sit in pews with their names embossed on little brass plates, their children away at private schools.

Lewis Ray, you have to do it. You have to show Turner a path out of these dying hills. As long as one heart beats, the friendship remains alive, and it's up to you now.

So, my friend, I will say farewell. Keep the faith.

I will see you in the stars.

Travis

I hugged my knees to my chest and buried my face in my folded arms. I listened for the rumble of the L&N carrying coal to the barges on the Big Sandy, but all I heard were the shrill cries of the cicadas. I tried to imagine folk having lunch at the Whip 'n Sip and Uncle Wallace cleaning another windshield at the Phillips 66, and Dakey at the Blue Star, cigarette bobbing with her every word, but all I could see were the stilled folded hands of Travis Wicker. I desperately longed for tears that would wash away my grief, but I was as dry as the creek beds of dog days.

"I thought I'd find you here."

It was the voice of Travis, who always came to me at the rock just when I needed him most.

"I'm Turner, Turner Wicker. Travis's son."

"I'm sorry," I said, looking around at him. "I'm Lewis Ray."

"I know who you are. I was hoping you would come."

✳ ✳ ✳

Even though I had planned to head back to Nashville that afternoon, I checked in to the Rest Haven, a motel between Stone Coal and Bosco. Just like the Roger Miller song, there was no phone, no pool, and no pets, but my small room did have a noisy air conditioner that blew cool air and circulated the smell of mildew around. I spent some time the next two days visiting with Mamma Lou and Annie and her family. When I ate, I had breakfast or lunch with Gracie at the Dixie. But most of the time I spent by the fresh mound of dirt in the graveyard overlooking Stone Coal.

On the third day I headed back to Nashville. In Bosco I stopped at the only remaining pay phone in the county.

The phone rang three times.

"Hello."

"Hey. It's me. I'm heading home."

"How was it?"

"It was okay."

"Be careful. I love you. I'll see you tonight."

"Kissimmee?"

"Yes?"

"I have someone with me I want you to meet."

The End